The Risk of a Fall

For J.S.
Thank You.

One

The Granddaughter

The Grandma that I will always keep in my heart is the one who loves gardening and shopping at thrift and antique stores. She is the woman that has been strong enough to live the last 15 years without the man she still calls her husband, though he has been dead a long time. It was their house that I will remember going to every Friday after elementary school and the way it smelled when Pop was baking bread. I will remember that she is the one who encouraged me to get a studded belt when I was in Middle School, because it was, as she said, cool. She is the one who always thought I was smart, even though on the whole she felt men were smarter than women.

She could be hard around the edges sometimes, but I loved the glint in her eye when she was recounting stories of her spunky life. She is the one who can grow orchids by (supposedly) ignoring them. And she is the one who loved to throw parties on the fourth of July. Her home was always welcoming to anyone who visited. She could reuse a bread bag five times so she wouldn't be wasteful. She smelled like Chanel powder, because my grandfather used to buy it for her and it is the one "indulgence" she kept up after he was gone. She was the one who said she was going to wash her teeth instead of brush them. And she was the one who always had a hole cut in her right shoe to let the pressure off her bunion. She is the one who could recall the name of every cousin and every baby ever remotely related. She is the one who still got Christmas cards from people she met decades ago.

I love that Grandma. I love the part she has played in my life. And I loved the Sundays spent sitting talking at her dining room table. That is my grandma before dementia, strokes, brain tumors, cognitive dysfunction, and near-death oxygen deprivation altered her for good. That is my grandma before lawyers helped her try to charge me with unlawful imprisonment. I miss her, but I am glad to have had her for as long as I did.

Two

The Granddaughter

I got the call in the middle of the morning at work. Our family phone tree is a thing to behold. Before the doors closed on the ambulance, a neighbor called my Uncle Billy's wife, Sarah, who then called me.

So within 20 minutes of my grandmother falling in the road with her dog, I am on the road driving the hour between my town and hers. The last time I was needed to handle Gram's medical care was three years ago when I took her to an appointment at her vascular doctor and he made us drive straight from his office to the hospital. Or we were supposed to anyway; Ireene made me take her home first to "collect a few things" and make sure the dog could go to Uncle Billy and Aunt Sarah's house (*of course* the dog could go to Uncle Billy and Aunt Sarah's house, for years Ireene has been making every single family member promise to take care of her dog if something were to happen to her. That dog has about five potential homes).

Still, I have that achy feeling in my chest that I get when something bad is happening. Especially something that requires me to be vigilant and make sure my Gram gets the best care. That last time she was in the hospital, the attending surgeon asked me if we really wanted to do the surgery the vascular doctor scheduled? Because, he said, she is old and is going to die of something. It was a bit hard to trust him after that.

Five years ago, after my father died, Ireene asked me to be the one who "takes care of things after she dies". I've often thought how hard it must be for her to have to entrust so much of her life to someone for whom she used to change diapers. She has been telling me every Sunday for the last five years how she needs to get around to cleaning out closets so that when she dies, I will have less house to pack up. On our Sunday visits, we sit at her dining room table, her on the end with one hand patting her dog, Michael and I next to each other in front of her. Sometimes our little dog comes with us and sits on Ireene's lap while we talk. Animals have always loved this woman. I tell Ireene not to worry about the closets, we'll deal with that when the time comes.

She always asks if I'll let Uncle Billy come and help with some of the packing. He had an accident years ago that left him mostly blind, with little short-term memory, and in constant need of care. In some ways he is child-like, but he still has the same crazily large vocabulary and verbose way about him as he did before the accident, it is just that now his conversations are often laced with confusing embellishments that aren't based in reality. And unfortunately, his personality is now punctuated by a mean streak that doesn't seem to need a reason to show itself. I don't really remember him being hateful before his accident, but it has definitely become part of his character since.

He cannot drive or even leave his house alone. He knows enough to realize that he would be the one to take care of things for Ireene if his brain had not gotten damaged in the accident. As it is, Ireene is left with me. And every week I promise to make sure Uncle Billy helps when the time comes to pack up her house.

Michael promises too. Gram feels better when there is a man involved in things. She has always believed that men are better at "taking care of things", though she is careful to add that she knows I'll be good at taking care of things too, because I'm my father's daughter.

My father's other daughter, Betty, is also on Gram's legal paperwork. She lives in Tennessee. She'll come out if we need her, but mostly we are both on there so that one person (me) doesn't have to make decisions alone.

I laugh thinking that Ireene truly doesn't think we'll ever have to do anything. I firmly believe that the only reason

Ireene agreed to have a medical surrogate at all is because she imagines she'll never need one. She is in control of her life and she doesn't plan for that to change. Her plan is to die quickly and peacefully in her house one day.

I need to get to work. I pull my phone back out and call my mom and Betty. By the end of the hour-long drive, I'm certain that every living member of our family has been notified by *someone* that Ireene is headed to the hospital. When the 96-year-old matriarch of the family goes to the hospital, it is something people want to know. Besides the fact that Ireene has lived in the same house since 1970, and has walked her dog (four different ones by now) every single day of that. The entire neighborhood knows her as "the greyhound lady". So I am sure that the house-to-house grapevine is buzzing too.

When I get to the hospital waiting room, my cousins Jay and John, who I call Aunt Jay and Uncle John, Uncle Billy and his wife, Sarah, are there and they tell me that Ireene's hip is definitely broken and she is in surgery now. The five of us settle in to wait. Well, Billy doesn't really settle in, he is restless and paces. Which doesn't work all that well since he is about 80% blind. He has one spot in his right eye that he can see out of. Everything else is fuzzy black. So pacing for him involves a lot of bruised shins. And he doesn't really pace out of worry. His brain damage left him lacking in the ability to have personal connections. He paces more out of boredom and the anxiety of being in an unfamiliar place than because of any sense of foreboding about his mother's condition.

I, on the other hand, am totally worried because I know how bad hip surgery can end up for someone as old as Gram. The reason I know how bad it can be is that my sister quoted me the mortality stats of it on the phone on the way here. She can always be relied on to have random bits of trivia at the ready.

I stopped at home on my way here from work and got the file that holds my power of attorney, medical surrogacy, and a few other legal documents, and a spiral notebook so that

I can take notes when the doctors come talk to us. I learned last time with Dr. She'll-Die-of-Something that I should write down everything.

Three

Ireene

As I sit in this hospital bed, waiting, all I can think is "damn". I'm not usually the kind who swears. My late husband used to turn a colorful phrase or two, but it was never for me. But sitting here, that is all I can think of, just "damn". I'm ninety-six years old and I've made it this long living on my own and not being bothered in my own house. Then this had to go and happen.

It is the house we, my husband Henry and I, bought for $36,000 in 1970 when he retired. The original house was blown away in a tornado, but we put one up in its place, and that is where I live. I may move slow and be a little forgetful sometimes, but I take care of myself. I do my own gardening (up 'till last year I used the electric hedge trimmers, but they made me give that up) and I clean my own house. The top shelves may not get dusted as often as they used to, but I'll be darned if someone else is going to come in to my house and clean around me when I'm perfectly capable of doing it myself. They are always trying to get me to stop doing.

I'm sitting here in the middle of my thought when she comes in. As soon as she gets her foot in the door I tell her, "They said I can go home tomorrow." My granddaughter looks at me like I'm a daft little child and says slowly, "Gram, you actually have to go to rehab before you can do anything else. I got some information on the different options. Let's look at them and you can pick which one you want me to call to get you set up."

Humph. I don't want any of the three. So I say, "*Who says* I have to go to rehab?" Doctors. They didn't tell me that. Why would they tell me I can go home and tell her I can't?

I don't need rehab; I can get around just fine. I must

have said that out loud, because now my granddaughter is saying, "Gram, you could get around great before a few days ago. But since you broke your hip and they had to do surgery, walking will be hard until you get back up again through rehab." Don't see the point and I want to tell her that, but what I say is, "I have to get home to walk the dog and I can't afford rehab."

I'm watching her lips move and hear a couple things about Medicare, but my hearing aid batteries are low and it sounds like I'm hearing through wet cotton balls. My mind starts to wander and I'm thinking of Henry again. He was such a looker.

Henry and I got married on July 4, 1942. He was in the Army Air Corps and was stationed in Alabama; I drove all the way from New York to Alabama with a girl friend to meet him there. We had to drive with our headlights half blacked out at night, like everyone did back then because of the war. It made the drive a bit slow going, but we made the best of it. Even had a hand gun under the seat just in case! People never would have thought that about two young women. I never was one to shy away from an adventure. I couldn't have worked in New York City as a young woman if I'd been the skittish type. Took the train every day.

My mother made wonderful clothes. We didn't have much, but she could sew anything. I had a beautiful wardrobe of suits she made. For our wedding I wore one of the suits, one that I'd only worn once before so that it was more special. One of the young soldiers got a cake that someone had given him to celebrate his birthday. He was young, nineteen I think. Such a nice kid, Andy. I got a letter from him this last Christmas. He is the only one of the group still alive besides me, so he keeps up with me now and then. Well, Andy shared his birthday cake with us, so it was a little like having a wedding cake. Vanilla. It didn't matter that we didn't have a real wedding cake. Or that for years, we shared base housing with two and three other couples to a house. We always had each other. And we knew how to throw a party!

Four

Ireene

I just woke up and am feeling confused. They're telling me I'm going somewhere, but I'm not sure where. I need a comb. I can't let people see me without combing my hair. I reach for my teeth on the bedside table, and a nurse comes over to help. Just as I'm saying, "I don't need any help," I get a searing pain through my hip when I try to sit up. The nurse pushes a button behind my head and buzzes the top of my bed so I can sit up better. I ask her where I'm going and she replies, "Well I don't know where you are going, Honey. But someone will be up to talk to you in a bit and they'll have discharge papers." Yes! Discharge papers. I'll sign the discharge papers, call a cab, and be home by dinner. I hope my neighbor is taking care of my dog.

It was the dog that got all this mess started. But it isn't his fault, he is just energetic. My Mars is a beautiful greyhound. Everyone says he is too much for me to handle. He gets exuberant sometimes and jumps up on me. My skin is a little thin and I bleed a lot, so it always looks worse than it is. One of the times he knocked me down I got this great bruise from derriere down to the back of my knee. It was fun to lift my shorts leg up to show people! Nothing risqué, mind you, just enough get a reaction. Since I'm old they expect me to be boring.

Once last year I fell off the ladder to my attic and hit my head on my car that was parked close by. Tore up my arms and legs some and got a big bump on my head, but it wasn't that big a deal. Everyone acted like I would die any minute. Thought I might have a concussion or bleeding in my head. I just knew they would fuss, that is why I didn't call anyone when it happened. Just let them find out the next week when they came to visit. Did have a big gash of skin

10

peeled back on my leg, but my neighbor Willa, she's a medium that talks to dead people you know, she put some honey on it every day for a month and it healed up with just a bit of a scar.

Anyway, this time when Mars got spooked by a passing car, his leash wrapped up my legs and I went down. Now, I can take pain. Always have had a hearty constitution. When I was pregnant if I was feeling a little nauseous, I just ate a tomato out of the garden and that fixed me right up. Never had another problem. I don't understand these girls today who complain about every little thing. Even after the tornado I had a pin in my elbow and you didn't see me complaining (oh that tornado - you should have seen my husband that night flying through the air in his birthday suit when the roof came off!). So pain doesn't usually bother me, but I could tell this time there was something really wrong with my hip. Then I saw neighbors running to come help me and I knew I wouldn't be able to get up and get home before their help landed me in the hospital.

Now here I am looking for a glass to wash my teeth in so I'm ready when the discharge papers get here and I can head home.

Five

Ireene

Well, they made me to go rehab. Apparently I don't have a say in these matters. Hospital policy, they said. Finally someone brought me batteries for my hearing aid, so at least now I can hear what people are saying (though sometimes I wish I couldn't). The old woman who shares my room is crazy and thinks that her last roommate murdered someone. Martha kept wailing about it all night. And she keeps climbing out of bed to find her stash of chocolate hidden somewhere in the room. But seeing as they have her tethered to the bed with an alarm, every time she gets out of bed it makes a god-awful racket that sounds worse than an air-raid siren! I try to tell my granddaughter about this when she comes, how crazy my neighbor Martha is, but she just looks embarrassed and keeps glancing at the curtain hanging between mine and Martha's beds. I have it closed because Martha is only about three feet from me and her husband sits there in a chair all day long. You would think the man had something to do at home instead of sitting around our room all day. I try to talk a little louder thinking maybe she is just not understanding me, but no matter how many times I try to tell my granddaughter about how crazy Martha is, she just keeps looking at the curtain like she is worried about something. I'm the one that should be worried; I'm the one that has to stay in this room with crazy Martha.

I don't really eat much anymore, and boy does that seem to get them riled here at the facility. How many times a day can they try to force me to eat? When I'm at home I eat ice cream and sometimes yogurt. That is the best way to get my pills down, especially that big pink one. My granddaughter is always trying to get me to drink that stuff, what is it called?

Oh, I hate it when I can't remember things. Ensure, that's it. That stuff is only for the old and infirm and I'm not about to start drinking it. At home I take my car once a day to the grocery store to get my supplies. My granddaughter keeps trying to get me to move to one of those expensive Assisted Living places. I keep telling her I can't afford it and she keeps telling me there are "programs" that can help. Programs. I know how much money I have and it isn't enough for one of those fancy places. I still pay all my own bills (well I did before I landed in here) and she can't tell me that I can afford something that I know I can't. I agreed to go look at a couple of them with her last year. I figured if I did that, then I could say I knew my options in case it ever came time that I needed to move. That seemed to make her happy for awhile. I did consider selling my house at one point, but I still have way too much to do there first. I have *years* of things to sort through.

The other thing she gets on about is my driving. She says macular degeneration in my eyes and numb feet from poor circulation make for bad driving. Says if I lived in one of those places, that they'd drive me where I needed to go and I could eat in their cafeteria so I wouldn't have to make my own food. But I know they wouldn't take me to my doctors' appointments, and my son Billy's house, and to the grocery store when I want. Sometimes I just like to take a drive downtown and go through the thrift stores. I used to drive to the mall, but it is too far for me now. Last time I went to the thrift store, I found a salt cellar in the shape of a swan for fifty cents! Can you believe that? Now I know that one of those fancy living places wouldn't take me to the thrift store. And I wouldn't want them sitting there waiting for me while I shopped anyway.

A few weeks ago I rear-ended a lady in her car when I was leaving the church parking lot. Really it was just a bump. The lady got out and screamed at me that I am too old to drive and have no business behind the wheel of a car. Her face was all twisted and angry. Then she got back in her car and sped off. I was getting out my insurance information to give her, but she didn't even take it - just yelled and left. She didn't even give me a chance to say anything. I didn't tell my granddaughter about it. I don't need her getting any more ideas.

Six

Ireene

Now I don't mean to be negative, but I'm getting a little tired of this place. I do like the young man who does my physical therapy twice a day though. I think he is one of those men that likes other men. But I don't judge about that. It isn't my business. He tells me every day how good I'm doing and how he can't believe how feisty I am for my age. This makes me feel proud that finally someone realizes I can take care of myself. I wish everyone else would be so sensible. And he talks loud enough. I get so tired of asking everyone to repeat what they say all the time. Why can't they speak loud enough the first time?

I hate having to go sit with all those old women to eat my dinner. Some of them just sit there and one of them even drools. I like it better when Billy or my granddaughter are here during dinnertime because then I can eat in my room. I don't belong here. And I'm dying to get home to have a proper happy hour. My neighbor, Willa, the one who has meetings with dead people, comes over every night when she's in town. Scotch for her, bourbon for me, and booze soaked ice cubes for Mars. I don't eat much anymore and I weigh less than I used to. At 95 pounds I can't drink like I once did, so now I don't drink bourbon at 4:30 like was Henry's and my practice. I'm much more careful. I just have a few glasses of white zinfandel from 4:30 until Willa comes over at 9 pm when we break open the hard stuff. I don't sleep much, so it is nice to have a friend to talk to at night. She told me once she wants my house and sometimes I wonder if that is why she pays so much attention to me. But I don't think that is it. She wouldn't bring me things she cooked and sit with me telling stories if we weren't really friends.

Here, the nurses keep flapping at me about walking on

my own. They say it is too soon after surgery and I could fall. Every day we have to have this argument. We go round and round and it makes me mad. I don't need some person I don't know (especially a man - and a black man at that! I think he is one of those Haitian people) standing over me while I'm trying to go to the bathroom.

I can't read very well because my eyes are a little off. I pretend they are fine when my granddaughter brings me bills to sign. It takes me a long time to sign my name now, but I do it. They need to know I'm still in control.

They make me see this young blonde girl every day. Occupational Therapy they call it. I really don't know why I have to go to Occupational Therapy - I haven't worked since we were in the ambulance corps in New York. She asks me all sorts of questions. She is trying to get me to go to their kitchen to make brownies. She says I can't go home until I can show that I can cook healthy meals for myself at home. Now if that don't beat the band! I don't make brownies at home, so there is no reason to make them here. And since when are brownies healthy? I've been doing for myself for 96 years, why do they think I can't all of a sudden now?

They keep trying to get me to say I'll move to one of those Assisted Living places when I leave here. But I won't do it. My granddaughter is my medical representative, but only if I were to be incapacitated. And I'm not, so I'm going home.

Seven

Ireene

I used to be 5'7" and people said I looked like a blonde Rita Hayworth. Now when I look in the glass I wonder who the old woman is. She not only looks like a wrinkled gargoyle, but she moves things around my house and hides them so I can't find them. But back then, I was beautiful. I keep Henry's and my wedding picture on my nightstand so I can remember us as we used to be. He was so handsome and so smart. There wasn't anything he couldn't do. When I look around my house I see drapes that he sewed, a stained glass lampshade that he made, and wooden model airplanes in the shape of the B17 Bomber he flew in the Army Air Corps. I even have a little bottle of sand he sent me from Iwo Jima. The note he wrote said, "A little bit of Iwo", and I taped it on the outside of the bottle, along with the stamp from the envelope. Both are yellowed now, but my memory of receiving it is still clear. I don't need any of those things to have Henry with me every day though. Sometimes I talk to him. If I can't find something or am having a particularly difficult day, I ask him for some help.

I think it works too, because when I lost my engagement ring a few years back and couldn't find it for days, I was frantic. It isn't a real diamond, so it isn't worth anything, but I still couldn't bear the thought of losing it. I looked in between shirts in my dresser drawers, I checked the sink in case it came off while I was doing the dishes, and I checked the desk drawers where I'd been paying bills. Nothing. Finally one day I asked Henry to help me find it. That may sound silly. But the next morning when I opened my closet to get out my shoes, there was my engagement ring stuck in the sliding door track. It just sat there winking at me in the sunlight. I looked up and said thank you to my Henry.

When I was pregnant with my first child, we were stationed at a base in Idaho. Henry was at pilot school, and I was on my own. We hadn't been there long when Halloween rolled around. I love Halloween and just because I was alone didn't mean I was going to miss out. So I rooted around Henry's footlocker until I came up with an olive drab canvas flight suit that would close over my pregnant belly. Then I put on a gas mask I'd found, made a pillowcase into a candy sack, and went trick-or-treating. Maybe the neighbors thought I was strange or maybe they thought I was a stitch. But I sure looked a sight!

We had three children, all who had Henry's eyes. Dark brown and intelligent. Two of them are gone now. I have one son left, Billy. I try to see him every week. He had an accident years ago that left him not quite the same. He can't take care of himself anymore. To give his wife a rest, I go over one day a week and dust and do laundry. He needs me.

Eight

The Granddaughter

Walking down the hall to Gram's room, I'm thinking, "I hope Gram is in an okay mood tonight." I'm feeling pretty drained from the last few weeks of dealing with hospitals, rehab facilities, insane amounts of paperwork, the improper administration of medicines, lack of communication between night staff and day staff, and the new job I've had for only three months. Living an hour from here is taking its toll. I had no idea all of the things that can go wrong in places like this. It seems like it has gotten a bit better since we set up for the nurse to call me every morning at 6 am to tell me how Gram did overnight. We started that when Ireene began having nighttime episodes. She gets panicked and believes that the staff at the rehab center is trying to kill her. She screams and threatens to call the police. Each morning she remembers what happened and apologizes to whichever nurse's aide she railed against in the night.

They say because of her "advanced age" that such hallucinations are common after surgery and when beginning a stay at a nursing home. Plus she got a few infections that made things worse. Even so, not too many of us are used to strangers waking us up several times a night to poke and prod and give us pills. Add age and some ever-present confusion and I can see why it would be stressful.

For the first few weeks she was here, she was always worried that I spent too much time here. Mostly her worry came out in the form of berating, but the intent was the same.

Her nurse passes me and tells me Ireene did "just fine today". I look into Gram's room and see her sitting on the edge of her bed, waving her fork in the general direction of the dinner plate that sits on the rolling table next to her bed. It sits at a slant because it is piled halfway on top of a pack of tissues and Gram's grey faux-leather glasses case. It almost looks like she is talking to someone, but there is no one else in the room. There are tissues on the floor and magazines fanned out across the bed. The magazines tell me my uncle has been here. His wife, Sarah, drives him, and Gram's dog, here every day at least once to visit. When it comes to Billy, Sarah is as close to a saint as I'll probably ever meet. She has been with my uncle for 20 years. The last eight have been more in the role of caretaker than spouse. But she keeps going, taking care of him, and always being good to Ireene.

Uncle Billy wants to be helpful and so he brings Ireene old magazines each time he visits her here in rehab. But Gram's eyes have gotten so bad that she can't read without tilting her head sideways and putting the paper up close to her nose, almost like you would if you were trying to see dust on the surface of a desk. Tilt your head and get down to its level and look across the plane of the desk. That's how Gram reads now. I've seen her do it at her house. Since the day after her surgery, she's been campaigning for why she will continue driving when she gets home from rehab, and my guess is that she thinks if no one sees her read in that position, they'll think she can see just fine to drive. So the magazines sit unopened.

When I visit I generally bring Gram things she wants from the store. Sometimes she gets something stuck in her head and she can't seem to let it go until I bring it to her - hence why I've bought her new bras, fuzzy socks with grips on the bottom, nightgowns, and various other items. She has all those things at home, but she wants new ones. This is very un-Ireene; she never spends money and is always frugal. I've saved receipts for everything I've bought that she asked for, because she insists I not spend my own money but use hers. I show her the bills I've been paying from her bank account, so she stays involved in everything, because that is the way she wants it, to be involved. She always waves away the receipts and says, "I trust you!"

She gives directions on making sure we keep up with the lawn and pool service. She tells me these things each and every time I visit. Being in here gives her a lot of time to obsess over small details, and her forgetfulness makes her think she hasn't told me before.

I bring her calendar so she can make sure she keeps track of birthdays she doesn't want to miss (or have me keep track of the birthdays!). I tell her that no one would expect her to send birthday presents while she is in rehab. But she doesn't want to let anyone down. So I shop for birthday presents, wrap and ship them, and then report back to Ireene, then she can feel good about having done something for everyone's birthdays.

Aunt Jay and I share the task of keeping track of Ireene's doctors' appointments. Who knew you still had to go see your own doctors when you are staying in a medical facility? Aunt Jay and Uncle John own a business here in the town where Ireene lives and Aunt Jay has been able to take the time off to see Ireene every single day since she broke her hip. Knowing Jay can get here every day makes me worry much less. She and Uncle John have been stopping by to check on Ireene's house every day, because it makes Ireene feel better, and picking up the mail each day to give to me at the end of the week so I don't have to stop at the house, I can just go directly to see Ireene. Ireene even requests that they put her flag up every morning and take it down every night. They drive over just to do that. Ireene says her neighbors would be disappointed not to see her flag up after so many years. If it had been me, I would have just left it up, but Ireene is adamant that it not be up overnight. She also has them turn on her porch light each night. This little old lady sure knows how to make a bunch of grown people jump through whatever hoops she asks! It is just easier to do these things than to watch her obsess and worry over them. The only problem is…each thing we do for her is like a checkmark off her worry list and it frees her up to find something else for us to do, and then she obsesses and worries over that instead.

Since I am the one who is mainly responsible for her care, I've become the organizer and keeper of details, and when necessary, I am the bearer of bad news. Yesterday when I visited, I had to tell Gram that her last living cousin had died. She had been asking me all week to call the cousin for her birthday, wanted me to dial and let Ireene talk from the phone in her room. She took the news well, as she always does. When you're 96 years old, you get pretty used to having everyone you know die. But I felt horrible for having to tell her about yet another loss. She and I traveled to my father's funeral five states away when Gram was 91. And we viewed his body together with my sister, Betty. Since then, Gram and I have had a way of dealing with death together.

So as I come in tonight, I'm hoping she'll be feeling alright and not be too sad. I sit down in the side chair and say hello.

"How has your day been?" I ask.

"Oocknnam. Writing."

"I'm sorry Gram, I missed what you said?"

"Bshaaverba tatem ooglak."

Ireene is looking at me perfectly calmly like everything is fine. She thinks she is answering my question.

"Are you ok, Gram? Did something happen today that is making you have a hard time?"

"Cal..en...dar. Ooock. Ooock. Nable."

Now I'm starting to worry a bit.

"Did Uncle Billy come see you today?" I try.

"Able whoot bbummp. Bill."

I try a few more questions with the same results. Then I say, "Gram, I'm just gonna go out in the hall for a minute and I'll be right back." I'm impressed with how calm my voice sounds, because in my head I'm freaking out. I wonder how long she has been like this without any of the staff noticing. I find a nurse and tell her that Ireene doesn't seem to be able to speak, that just gibberish is coming out. The nurse bustles in and asks Ireene a few questions, "What day is it? Who is the president? Do you know your name?" She gets the same type of answers that I got, complete gibberish that sounds like it is coming from a faulty drive-thru speaker. The nurse says, "I'm going to call 911 to get an ambulance here to take Ireene to the hospital."

We get Gram sitting back in her bed and seemingly comfortable. I tell her that she is going to go to the hospital for some tests. She looks at me like I have a screw loose. I go outside to call the family, starting with John and Jay, and tell them we're going to the hospital. They say they'll meet me there; I know in part for Gram and in part so I don't have to be alone. Then I cry. I've had to handle awful stuff before, but this time the awful stuff is happening to my Grandma, and that just makes it harder somehow. Feeling that I am somehow responsible for the outcome of everything feels like a dark weight. I'm sitting on a bench in a garden area and try not to look conspicuous when a nurse's aide walks by on her break. Then, though I never understood how it is supposed to help, I stopped in a bathroom and splashed water on my face so Ireene wouldn't see that I'd been crying.

As I get back to the room the EMTs are arriving to load Ireene up. The nurse gives them the update that Ireene has lost speech, etc. The EMT says loudly to Ireene, "Do you know who the president is?"

Ireene answers, "A black man. Give me a minute. I voted for him even though I'm Republican. Obama. That's his name."

Then she proceeds to tell him that she was in the volunteer ambulance corps in New York before she and my grandfather retired.

Nine

Ireene

Something is wrong. It is evening and my granddaughter is here. She is sitting in front of me looking worried and asking me to repeat things. When I look at her I see my own blue eyes looking back at me with concern. She looks a little panicked and I can't figure out why. But I'm sure she is overreacting. I'm answering her, but every time I say something, she looks worse. She leaves and comes back with a nurse who is also asking me questions. Then everyone is poking and prodding me and flashing lights in my eyes.

This seems like it takes so long, but it is still night and my granddaughter is still here. Things feel cloudy and I can't seem to keep track of time. Then the ambulance men come in. One of them is a good looking young man. I tell him I was in the volunteer ambulance corps for many years in New York and I can tell he is impressed.

Ten

The Granddaughter

By the time we got to the ER, Ireene was completely out of it again. She wasn't talking gibberish, she just wasn't talking. Aunt Jay and I stayed in the ER with Ireene and talked about the most inane things, just to have something to do. It is odd the tone you adapt when around a very sick person. Everything is said quieter than normal, but is infused with a forced happiness that is intended not to cause the person more distress. I think someone should do a study of the family members, 'cause I'm guessing that the effort of always trying to adapt that "pleasant and unworried" tone causes more stress to the family members doing it than it causes good to the patients it is supposed to benefit.

After a few tests, the ER doctor asked us if we knew Ireene has two brain tumors. Then he says the speech problem probably meant that she was having a stroke while she was trying to talk. I'd known about one of the tumors, but not that there were two. I don't even think Ireene knew that. She's joked for years that the tumor in her head is what makes her memory so bad. The way she described it, it wasn't a "bad" tumor, just more of a dead space. I'm pretty sure that she viewed having "dead space" in her head as a funny quirk.

Up until today, all conversations with the doctors involved Ireene. I was there, but I always tried to direct them to talk to her. She gets REALLY mad if the doctors talk to me and not her, so I always try to head that off at the pass. But tonight, she laid on the gurney with her eyes open while the doctor said we should be prepared for the fact that there is nothing more to do now and we just need to make Ireene comfortable until the end. I'm pretty sure she couldn't even hear him.

I was so glad Aunt Jay was there talking to him with

me, because then we had to go out to the waiting room and tell Uncle John, Uncle Billy, and Sarah. I was glad Jay heard the doctor say there is nothing more to be done, so this revelation wouldn't be on my shoulders alone.

Then we called a medical van to bring Ireene back to the rehab, which also happens to be a nursing home, where we will arrange for her status to change from rehab to palliative care. Gram will stay in the same room and everything.

I'm in my car following the medical van and I call my mom on the way from the hospital back to nursing home. It is almost 2 am, but I know she'll want the update. I feel exhausted from a full day at work and then this emotional evening. Mom asks me if Michael is coming down to meet me.

It has only been a few years since his very young first wife died slowly and painfully from cancer. The years he spent taking care of her while his heart was breaking have left an imprint of sadness on him that will always be there. He is a wonderful human being who has found his happiness again, so I will do anything I can to keep from renewing the hurt. I decided right away on the day that Ireene first went to the hospital that I wasn't going to subject him to places and situations that would force him to think again and again of his late wife's pain.

"No," I tell Mom, "he'll stay home and take care of the dog. He's had enough hospital vigils for one lifetime."

Eleven

The Granddaughter

That was two days ago. It is now midnight and I'm driving down to the nursing home. I just got off the phone with the nurse who called to say Ireene's vital organs are shutting down and she believes Ireene will be gone by morning. The nurse asked me to come and to bring Ireene's cremation information with me, so that when Ireene passes, they will be able to call to have her body collected.

I head down the quiet hallway that is usually filled with people in wheelchairs, and see the family all sitting in the hall outside Ireene's room. The nurse tells them what she told me on the phone. Aunt Jay tries calling around to find a Catholic priest to administer the Last Rites, but none are available. We go in one by one and say our goodbyes to the unresponsive Ireene. Then we sit in the hall, waiting, and start to organize what needs to be done. I sit in her doorway so I can talk to them and be with her at the same time, because I don't want her to be alone.

The hours pass and it seems better to keep busy and make plans than simply to sit. My job is so new that I don't have a lot of time off. It is Friday and I'll have to get as much done as possible this weekend so I don't have to take more time off next week. I'm so lucky they've let me have this much time already. The family says now that of course they will help with everything about the house and Gram's belongings too. Uncle Billy just wanders the halls and looks for a snack.

Ireene doesn't want a memorial service. She says none of us go to church with her while she is alive, so why should we go to church for her after she is dead?

Twelve

Ireene

I can't see anything. I can't move, can't talk. I try to say something, but nothing happens. Mostly I just hear buzzing and then silence. Now I hear murmuring, like someone is talking far away. I could swear someone just said something about Last Rites and cremation. I wonder vaguely if my roommate is dying. But I'm really too tired to think about it now.

Thirteen

The Granddaughter

It's Saturday morning and the family just left. I'm going to stay for a few more hours, at least until one of them comes back to relieve me. I'm sitting on a folding chair behind the curtain that has been pulled around Ireene's bed. The lights are off, and thankfully the roommate, Martha, went home yesterday. I'm watching Ireene's chest rise and fall as she breathes in and out. Every few minutes it seems to pause, like her body is forgetting to breathe for a bit, before it starts again. I find myself holding my breath each time that happens.

It is quiet in here other than when aides come in every hour and yell, "Hello, Ireene, how are we doing? Let's take your blood pressure!" And so on and so on and so on. I wish they would stop that. I have this image in my head of my grandmother's soul getting close to being ready to go wherever it is that souls go, then getting jolted back into her body every time one of the aides shouts at her. The nurses have said Ireene will die soon, but apparently the aides have made it their mission to keep that from happening.

My mind wanders back to three days spent sitting in the trauma unit waiting room the year my step-sister died. She'd had a life of 40 years filled with mental anguish and physical abuse that ended with her shooting herself in the stomach with a shotgun. My guess is that she was attempting to shoot herself in the chest, but the angle or recoil caused an unfortunate direction that made the shot take out one side of her intestines, her pelvis, and the top of her right leg. Hundreds of little silver balls embedded deep into her flesh.

It took three days for her to die. She bled and she bled. I never saw her, and I am glad. I was in the waiting room with her brother and Betty while my father and step-mom were at her bedside. To date, that had been the most horrifying thing

I'd dealt with…being with my step-brother when they finally turned his sister's machines off.

All of this with Ireene is hard in a different way. I wasn't close to my step-sister, but my grandmother I'd lived within a mile or two of my entire life. For my step-sister, my presence was more for "moral support" for the others, where with my grandmother, I feel that my role is to be here to see her through everything that happens, whatever that may be. If her sons can't be here for her, then I will make sure that I am.

I'm one of those people that if I don't know about something, I'll research it to death until I do. I have an article in my bag that I printed from the internet after that night in the hospital a few days ago. I hoped it would help me understand what is coming. It was written by a nurse, Angela Morrow, RN. It says the journey to death often starts one to three months prior to the actual death. Some people may withdraw from their surroundings and start to revisit old memories. They may have a reduced appetite and weight loss, but their body chemistry changes so they do not feel hungry. One to two weeks prior to death, they begin to sleep more often, and they may have hallucinations of and speak to people who have already died. The hallucinations may include things like fearing hidden enemies or feeling invincible. They may make aimless motions. Blood pressure lowers and lips and nail beds may take on a bluish tint.

The person may have a surge of energy just hours before death, possibly even eating again after having had no interest in food. Breathing becomes slowed, and there may be congestion in the airway. Lips and nail beds turn bluish purple. The person may become unresponsive; they may have their eyes semi-open but not see their surroundings. They may have periods of rapid breaths followed by periods of not breathing. Eventually breathing will cease. It is hard to read and to think about what is coming, but strangely, it actually makes me feel a little bit better to have an idea about what is happening to Ireene.

Later Jay, Billy, and I will go to Ireene's house to start going through her things. For as long as I've been alive, Ireene has been putting masking tape on the bottom of everything in her house. Each piece of tape has a person's name on it, the person she wants that item to go to when she dies. She also wrote me a six page letter several years ago listing out everything else in the house that is not marked with tape. She said she never wanted there to be any question where every single thing went, so she wrote it all out ahead of time. Practical as always.

So Jay, Billy, and I plan to go organize things (mostly Jay and I plan and Billy just agrees) in the house so they are easier to remove when the time comes, thinking that organizing well and making the most of our weekend time is the best plan to start accomplishing everything that will need to be done. I guess it is easier to focus on that than on the dying process that is slowly playing itself out.

Fourteen

Ireene

For some reason someone is holding me in a sitting position when I want to be laying down. Someone is holding a straw to my lips, and I am so thirsty, but no matter how hard I try I can't swallow. My throat won't work. My mouth and throat feel sticky and like they are glued in place. I can't open my eyes.

"Ireene, can you hear me?" I think I mumbled something. I know a sound came out. Finally they let me lay back down again.

A very happy feeling floods me because I am sitting next to my mother at our home in New York. She has her sewing machine set up next to me and she is holding a pearl button between her teeth while she threads a bobbin. She is telling me about her week at work. Her boss at the talent studio said Clark Gable is coming in next week. Oh, wouldn't that be wonderful!

My grandfather comes into the room and asks me how school was today. This is my favorite part of the day. Mom and I live with Grandma and Grandpa and he always comes home from work and asks me about school. I love to look at his wrinkly face. I try to get up so I can put my feet on top of his shoes and dance with him around the kitchen, but something seems to be holding me back from touching him.

Fifteen

Ireene

I am awake now, though I feel like I am really still sleeping, and my granddaughter is sitting next to me holding my hand. She is saying, "Gram, it is okay if you need to go. You have taken care of our family our whole lives. We all love you so much. And we understand if you need to go."

"Do you think anyone would be angry with me if I died?" I ask her. My voice still sounds sticky and raspy, but she is sitting close to me, so she understands.

"No Gram. Everyone loves you and wants what is best. Don't worry, we'll all take good care of each other. And we'll take care of Uncle Billy. You don't have to worry. It is alright to go now if you are ready." I think it is strange that she is almost whispering, but I can hear her just fine.

Then we just sit. She pats my hair and I look at the ceiling.

I must have fallen asleep for a while. As I start to wake up now, I see Henry sitting next to me. I reach out to touch his face, but I can't feel his skin. He is talking to me and I feel so happy. I just wish I could touch him.

I point him out to my granddaughter, "Do you see that your grandfather came to visit me?" I try again to touch him but can't quite do it.

Sixteen

Ireene

I don't know what day it is, but all afternoon my granddaughter has been holding the phone to my ear so people can talk to me. I hear from my granddaughter, Betty, and her mother, who I still consider my daughter though she was divorced from my son years ago. They both sounded like they were crying and kept telling me they love me. I told them I love them too.

I ask what's going on and my granddaughter tells me that it has been days since they had to take me to the hospital the last time. She says my hands had turned black and I was unresponsive (I look down at my hands and they look fine now). The nurses called the family because they believed I would not make it. She says something about a stroke.

"What!? I haven't had a stroke," I say.

"You hadn't had one before this week that we know of," she says, "But they think you had at least one, probably a few, a couple days ago."

Well that just makes me angry. She can tell me that all she wants, but I don't remember a thing about it. I say, "I don't know why everyone seems to expect me to die. I'm not ready to die."

I keep seeing shadows over her head and when I point them out to her, she acts like she can't see them. I try to touch them and can't reach. This is all so frustrating and wouldn't be happening if I were at home. And I have to use the bathroom.

Seventeen

The Granddaughter

Gram has been here for a couple of months now and she's moved on from worrying about birthday presents to worrying about Christmas presents. When I walked in earlier today, I had a dozen donuts for the nursing station. Gram has been giving them hell lately. She has been pretty paranoid and thinks everyone is out to get her. She tells anyone who will listen that she is going to call a cab and go home, or just walk out and down the road. The fact that she is still mostly in a wheelchair doesn't seem to dissuade her.

When I arrived with the donuts one of the nurses said, "We're so glad you are here." They never say that. Usually they are wary of me because I always want to know how Gram is doing, and since they gave her a medication she is allergic to, I always ask to see her daily meds too. Let's just say life is easier for them when their patients' families are not involved. So, I knew it had to be something big to make them happy to see me.

Ireene had an accident in her bed earlier in the day. She tried to get up on her own and walk to the bathroom to clean up but wasn't strong enough to get across the room. When an aide tried to help her, she went wild. She was barricaded in her room with her underwear around her ankles with feces on her bed, legs, arms, in her hair, and pooling in her slippers. She was trying to shove a chair in front of the door so the aide couldn't take her out of the room to the shower and get her cleaned up, but the door was stuck partway open. She scratched the aide on the neck. The aide who, until that point, had been Ireene's favorite and who was always sweet and went out of her way for Ireene. Ireene's new roommate was hunched on her side of the room with a look that was a cross between petrified and entertained. The room did not smell good.

Gram has been pretty mad at me lately. Each time I see her, she accuses me of lying to her - about having a stroke, about going to the hospital, about almost dying, about doing her bills, about Uncle Billy. It doesn't really matter what, she is just plain mad. And she tells me every chance she gets. She keeps asking me over and over what happened and why she is in the nursing home/rehab facility. She has decided that I am the reason she is here and if it weren't for me, she could be home and happy. So, I wasn't sure I was going to be able to help calm her down.

I was wrong. I called through the door of her room that I was here and was hoping to take a walk with her to the shower and that I didn't mind waiting for her while the aide helped her clean up. It was like a deflated toddler who has exhausted themselves after a particularly rigorous tantrum. The door opened fully and she let me in. She took my arm, and followed the aide with me, shuffling the 20 feet down the hall to the shower room. It made me so sad how she just seemed to deflate, and how she seemed to just need to know I was in the room.

When she was cleaned up and back in bed, exhausted, the staff and I started talking about moving her to a private room. No matter how good she thought she was doing, they were convinced that she was still in the stages of dying. They agreed to put her in a private room that was vacated earlier that day, and she would continue to be a palliative care client until she either passed away or got better enough to go back to rehab. But for now, they were going to put the bed and wheelchair alarm on her, like the one her first roommate, Martha, was wearing several months before.

Eighteen

The Granddaughter

Gram's 100 days on post-surgery Medicare are coming to an end and she'll have to leave here. Soon we're going to have to talk to her about selling her house. She has been talking about it for years, but it is one of those things that she thinks will never actually happen. She could have made twice its actual value if she sold it a couple of years ago when she first started talking about it. But now the value is back down to what is realistic, and she uses the "low" price as her reason for the delay.

It is Sunday and I've come down to try taking Gram out to lunch. The nursing staff decided to take Ireene off palliative care status and have her begin rehab again. They've said that since she doesn't seem to be getting worse, we should start trying to do things with her again. I try not to think the change of heart is because of the looming end to Medicare coverage. My medical surrogacy was activated the night Gram became incapacitated (though I'd been doing her paperwork and arrangements all along anyway), but it is now revoked as she is no longer incapacitated. So technically, she can make all her own decisions. The confusion, paranoia, near blindness, and trouble walking and doing things for herself are all apparently not a factor.

I was hoping this status change back to a rehab patient would make Ireene feel happier. Going back to rehabbing with the prospect of leaving this facility. Instead, she has started obsessing over where she will go next and how much money she has. It is nothing for her to bring the conversation up 10 or 12 times in an afternoon. It is like there is a faulty tape loop that just keeps replaying in her head.

I walk in to her room; the walls are covered with drawings from her grandchildren and nieces and nephews.

There is a painting of mine that we put on the wall; it is a flower and I thought maybe it would make her happy and remind her of her garden. The wedding picture of her and Pop is on her dresser. I'm holding my breath waiting to see which version of Gram I will see today, when she barks, "Why didn't you tell me!?" Oh shit.

"Why didn't I tell you what, Gram?" thinking it is going to be about breaking her hip and almost dying and having strokes, as those are generally her go-to questions.

"Why didn't you tell me that Henry is dead?" she says and then bursts into tears.

Double shit. I've never seen my grandmother cry. I'm 38 years old and I've not seen it once, even when each of her sons died. She believes crying is weakness and a. doesn't do it, and b. doesn't think other people should do it. When we arrived at my father's house to attend his funeral, it hit me that he wasn't in there. We pulled into the driveway and I got out of the driver's side. I stood there looking at his log cabin house, where his newly widowed wife was inside, and my eyes welled up. Ireene got out of the passenger seat, looked over at me, and said sharply, "What are you crying about?" When we viewed his body she wanted to know why the mole on his face looked weird. And during the memorial service, she didn't like the preacher (the preacher was Baptist, she is Roman Catholic) so she turned her hearing aids off and waited until she saw people get up signaling the end of the service to turn them back on.

So I don't have any experience with *this* grandmother, but I say, "Oh Gram, I'm so sorry. Pop has been gone for a long time. You do know that he's been gone, you are just having a hard time remembering because of the strokes you had." She looks confused and then says, "What about my mother? Your Aunt Jay was here earlier and said my mother is dead. Why didn't you tell me about that?"

I sit next to her and hold her hand, "Gram, I'm sorry you are feeling like this. Your mom has been gone a very long time. Think about it - how old are you? Ninety-six? Then it wouldn't really be possible for your mom to still be here, right? I'm sorry, because I know it feels like it just happened." She considers this and then says, "You still should have told me!"

She abruptly stops crying and says, "You are always keeping things from me. It isn't fair and I can't believe you would keep it from me that Henry died! I was wondering why he wasn't visiting me here anymore and Jay kept telling me he is dead. I told her, 'He was here yesterday! He isn't dead.'"

She is still sitting in her pajamas even though it was our plan to try going to lunch today. I tell her maybe we should skip lunch today and try another day. She looks angrily at me and I can't tell if it is because she thinks I didn't tell her Pop and her mom died, or because she is mad we aren't going to go out to lunch.

After sitting with Gram awhile, I leave. In my mind I'm comparing that conversation to the one we had the night when she was having strokes. I can't decide which was more heart-breaking. My conclusion? They both sucked royally.

Nineteen

Aunt Jay

I've been with Aunt Ireene all morning. I brought my grandkids with me yesterday, but I don't think I'll do that anymore. During dinner after our visit the kids asked me, "Why does Aunt Ireene yell at you so much?" They draw her pictures and do their best to be happy about visiting her. But when they are there, she scowls at them like they are in her way. And now they are upset because they think Aunt Ireene is mad at me.

So today I came by myself. I brought all the laundry I washed for Ireene. The nursing home will wash their patients' clothes, but Ireene doesn't like the idea of her clothes mixing with everyone else's, and I can't say I blame her. I updated her on how the family is doing, telling her that her out-of-town grandson would be coming for Christmas. I'd finished putting away her clothes and was making idle conversation when Billy's wife dropped him off. He is without the dog today, probably because Sarah couldn't stay to watch them both. As he sits down with Ireene I say, "I'm going to go outside and make a few phone calls for work. I'll be back in a few." They both nod and I walk out of the room. Halfway down the hall it hits me that I didn't bring my phone. So I turn around and walk back to Ireene's room. As I get close to the doorway I hear Billy say, "I told you not to give her authority over anything, but you didn't listen to me. So now you have to live with what she does." Whoa. I stop short and lean against the wall by the doorway to hear the conversation.

"You are fine and should be able to live wherever you want. She shouldn't be allowed to make you move someplace you don't want to," Billy says.

Ireene responds, "I know it. The nurses say it is my decision to make. But she says I have to go to a home. She is taking care of my house and paying my bills and doing my banking, so I need her. She can't stop doing those things and I think she will stop if I go back to my house. She said if I can go home that should mean I am able to do those things myself. You know, I love her because she is my granddaughter, but I don't really like her very much. I wish I didn't have to rely on her."

Crap. Figuring out all this stuff has been hard enough without Billy stirring the pot. The man has brain damage and can't take care of himself, so he is the last one that should be advising Ireene. Billy can't even remember if he's eaten breakfast and lives in a fantasy world most of the time. But he is the only child she has left, so she is going to cling to what he says. And he agrees with her about moving home, so she is going to cling to that too.

I can't decide if I should go in and get my phone or keep listening to hear what is going on with them. Ireene has been very paranoid for quite awhile now. I know some of it is from the strokes and oxygen deprivation, but I wonder if some of it isn't from alcohol withdrawal. When you've been drinking like she does your whole life, I'm guessing a few months without it can make you pretty cranky.

She thinks people are stealing from her. She thinks Lorna and I are conspiring against her. She thinks we move things around her room just to upset her. Doesn't matter that Lorna is her granddaughter or that I am her niece, Ireene thinks we are hiding things from her. Never mind that we tell her everything she wants to know *every* time we see her, but she forgets it again an hour later.

Ireene usually aims her comments by saying "they" made me to this, or "they" did that to me. Sometimes "they" might be rehab staff, sometimes "they" might be doctors, but lately "they" almost always means Lorna and me. The way she says it makes it sounds like it is *They* with a capital T. Like we have the power to manipulate her universe like some supreme being of evil.

I listen for a few more minutes before I enter the room and announce that I forgot my phone.

Twenty

The Granddaughter

Michael and I just picked up Gram and we're driving over to Aunt Jay and Uncle John's house for Christmas dinner. Ireene seems in good spirits, but after having heard about her and Uncle Billy's conversation about me from Aunt Jay, I'm finding it hard to take Ireene's pleasantness at face value. We drive in my car instead of Michael's because mine is low to the ground and Gram says it is easier for her to get into. That means Michael is folded into the back seat with Ireene's wheelchair, but he doesn't complain.

We get out and unload everything. I start pushing Ireene's wheelchair up to the house.

"I can walk, you know," Ireene says, irritable now.

"I know you can Gram, but we didn't bring your walker, only your wheelchair."

"Then I'll walk without it," she says. Mental sigh.

"Gram, look, the pathway is made of those unfinished stones. It would be very hard for you to walk on without falling on the rocks. Let's just use the chair for now, okay?" She doesn't answer, so I take that as a sign to keep going.

Once we get inside and everyone has hugged and oohed and ahhed at how well Ireene is doing, we get her settled in the family room next to the couch. Michael asks if she would like a drink, knowing that her answer will be wine. And it is. She looks at me, almost daring me to contradict her. I say nothing. I don't have to because we've already planned for this. Ireene is on about a trillion medications right now (the last addition is an antibiotic for yet another infection) and is in a nursing home; we didn't think it prudent to take her out and let her get drunk before we return her. So we'd bought non-alcoholic white zinfandel at Total Wine and put it in Jay and John's fridge the other day.

Michael brings her back a cold glass and she beams at him like he is her favorite person, which I guess compared to me right now, he is. She takes a sip and seems to visibly relax.

Ireene did pretty well all evening. For a number of years now she has been very quiet at family gatherings. She says so many people talking at once makes it hard for her to hear. So it wasn't out of the ordinary for her to sit with her wine just watching the goings-on. The kids opened their presents and ran to thank her; the look on her face told me she couldn't remember what I'd gotten them for her and was trying to hide that fact from the children.

We set her up to Skype with Betty, her two girls, and my mom in Tennessee, so they could say Merry Christmas. She talked to them for a couple of minutes before she started looking confused and retreating back into silence.

When we brought her back to the nursing home that night, she seemed tired but content.

Twenty-One

Ireene

I think my granddaughter left me. I haven't seen her all week. She hasn't called me. I know I can't hear to talk on the phone, but why hasn't she tried calling? Jay said something about her being sick, but I think that might be just an excuse. I think she just got tired of coming to see me.

Some of my neighbors were here earlier today and they can't wait until I get home. They can't believe how good I'm doing and don't think I need to go to one of those expensive Assisted Living places either. My mother visited this morning too. It has been a busy day for visitors!

Twenty-Two

The Granddaughter

I have been so sick for days. It is the worst time to be sick because Gram has to move out of the facility by next week. I need to talk to her about the options before our meeting with the rehab people to discuss her upcoming move. They'll have a nurse, an Occupational Therapist, and a social worker there. I can't call Ireene to talk about it, because she can't hear on the phone. I can't ask Aunt Jay to have the conversation with her alone, because that just wouldn't be fair. If I'm the one ultimately responsible, then it should be me that has to tell her that her house is halfway packed up and not in livable shape.

I just finished writing this letter and I'll call Jay and ask her if she will read it to Gram, since Gram has trouble seeing. It's not ideal, but it is the best I can do right now. She hasn't been able to keep any details in her head, so maybe having it written down she'll be able to refer back to it and it will help her remember later.

Wednesday, January 5

Dear Gram,

I am really sorry that I have been too sick to come see you. My respiratory infection just keeps hanging on, and I don't want to infect you with it.

Jay and I planned to come down and talk with you on Saturday, but since I can't be there, I thought I'd try writing things out to see how it goes. You and I have been through a lot together in the last three months, and I'm sorry I can't be sitting next to you for this conversation too. But I hope you know that as soon as I'm better, you can count on me to go through the next phase with you.

January 16th is the 100th day that you will have been in the nursing home. Medicare and your coinsurance pay up to that point. After January 16th, it is all private pay from there. So the timing is upon us to use the next two weeks to figure out where you should go from here.

I'll get back to that. But first, I need to catch you up on what's happened since you've been in the facility. I know you know some of the details by now. We waited this last week or so since the last of your infections cleared up just to make sure you were going to stay stable before we shared all this info with you, to make sure you were strong enough again. And even though you are strong again, I know some of it will be hard to hear, and I am sorry for that.

The short version is that, after your initially good response after your hip surgery, you started rapidly going downhill, sometimes losing your ability to speak, right around Thanksgiving. The decline was likely started because of a Urinary Tract Infection and a Respiratory Infection. Apparently, both are very common in post-hip surgery patients (and why I don't want to be near you while I have a respiratory infection right now). After two trips to the hospital and CT scans, they determined that you'd been having a series of small strokes that they called TIAs. They said the strokes and the infections were likely the cause of your delirium (hallucinations, confusion, dramatic mood swings).

On December 4th, the facility called the family and told us that you were unresponsive and that you were expected to not make it until morning. I know this is probably hard to listen to, but I need you to understand how things happened. That night, your vital signs were so low, that they had me give them your cremation details so they would have it for the next morning.

The next day you started responding a little bit. You couldn't open your eyes or swallow fluids, but you reacted to questions. During the next week, the staff's aim was solely to keep you comfortable. They put you in what is called Palliative Care status.

During that time, I spent most nights at your house, so I could be closer if you needed me. I also started preparing your house bit by bit to be packed up and eventually sold.

The family all met together and agreed that it was time to start packing things up so that we could be sure things went where you wanted them to go. I emptied the desk, the dressers, and things like that, packing some in boxes and leaving some out for later packing. Jay, Billy, and I spent a day together with the letter you had written out to me (the one on the yellow lined paper), separating everything in the china cabinet down by who you had either listed in the letter or written on the bottom of each item on masking tape. Then we went through the rest of the house and did the same thing with the big pieces of furniture (we've since moved a couple pieces of furniture out, but the rest are still there). The three of us, Billy, Jay, and I, did it together, so that we could be sure we got it right based on what you had written down and told each of us over the years. I think we did okay.

During that time, I also forwarded your mail to come directly to my house, so that I could get your mail daily instead of picking it up down there once a week.

It was just a few days later that you started to get better. You were still very confused for another week or so. I don't know if you remember, but it was a very hard couple of weeks for you. Each time I visited, I knew you were so frustrated with having to be in the facility and I tried to tell you what was happening as often as possible. But the details were coming in and out of focus for you and that was hard.

Just before Christmas I talked to the director of nursing at the facility and they agreed that you were no longer in the Palliative Care stage and would be put back in the regular "program" with doing physical therapy and such.

And you know the rest. Since shortly before Christmas, you've been doing great! I am so happy to see my Gram's spunk back! And now you know the details of why everyone keeps calling you "the miracle lady". You very nearly died, and then came back to us.

That brings us back to what happens now. There are a few factors:

1. I talked to the director of nursing and the head nurse of your wing at the facility and both recommend that you go to live in a "care facility". You don't need a nursing home, per se, but someplace where you are not isolated, so you have someone to help with medicine and to watch for signs of stroke, etc. - help when you need it, not when you don't.

2. Your mail is coming to me and I'm keeping track of your bills and your medical expenses, and I am happy to continue to do so forever if you like. Your house has everything down off the walls and most of the furniture emptied and has labels on most things

of where they should go. It isn't really in a shape that you could move back in, even if that were a good option.

I know that this is all a huge amount to deal with and think about. And if you want to take a couple days to sort out what you think, we have a little time.

There are a couple of options to consider, all of them involve putting your house on the market, but I know you've already been considering that possibility for several years. One option is that you can stay at the facility in the same room you are in. It is not cheap, but they would work with us on the finances using your monthly income and then supplementing when the house is sold and you have more available cash.

The other option is the place Jay has been telling us about called Swiss Flowers. It is a six room facility that is run by a lady that is a client of Jay and John's. I talked to her on the phone the other day and she sounds very nice. She is supposed to be sending me the information on their pricing, etc. If you decide you want to, maybe Jay and John could take you for a visit to Swiss Flowers to see what you think?

If you like it, they have a room open and you could move there between now and January 16th (assuming the pricing and payment part works, I'll get back to you when I know more about that).

And now that you are mobile again, Jay and I can take you over to your house to go through things. We can go as many times as we need to. You can get the things that you want to bring with you to either the facility or Swiss Flowers. You can check on the things that we divided and labeled to see if you want to change anything. And you can direct us in what to do with things that are *not yet packed or dealt with.*

That way you would be living in a safe place with people to look out for you if you need them, but you can still do the finalizing of things at your house the way you want them before it goes on the market.

Anyway, those are the best options we've come up with. I know none are ideal. But it sounds like the Swiss Flowers place is a smaller, more family environment where you wouldn't always have people popping in asking you if you want to play bingo (which I know you hate!).

I wish I could be sitting with you to talk about it. But we can try talking on the phone or maybe Jay can bring in her computer and set it up so I can talk to you like you talked on Skype to Betty and Mom on Christmas.

At any rate, that is the news to date. If there is anything you wanted to know that I didn't answer, just ask me.

I love you and am lucky to have you as my Gram. I'll get better soon and come down and help deal with all this "stuff".

Love,
Lorna

Twenty-Three

Aunt Jay

Ireene just finished reading the letter Lorna wrote her. She wasn't interested in having me read it to her. I wonder how much she read or how much she just skimmed over and if she really got what Lorna was trying to tell her. John and I are sitting here waiting for things to start flying, but all she says is, "Which pieces of furniture were moved out?" When we tell her, she just shrugs.

We arrange for me to pick Aunt Ireene up tomorrow and take her to see Swiss Flowers so she can see if she likes it or if she wants to look at other places. Ireene just looks tired and confused. John and I leave her alone to get some rest.

Twenty-Four

The Granddaughter

My cell starts ringing as Michael and I are carrying groceries up the stairs to our apartment. I put down my bags and fumble through my purse until I find it, pressing send just before voicemail takes over.

"Hi, it's Sarah. Everything is fine and there is no emergency. Are you in the middle of anything, or do you have a minute?" Sarah always starts her phone conversations this way. There has been so much drama in her life with Uncle Billy and more recently with Ireene, that she wants to assuage my fears by telling me right away that there is no emergency.

"No, I'm good. Just give me a second to get in the house," I respond. I grab my two bags off the ground and run up the last flight of stairs. I get in the apartment and drop everything on the floor.

"Ok, what's up?"

"Um. This is a little weird, but there is something I thought you should know," Sarah says.

I laugh, "What isn't weird with our family lately? Go ahead, hit me."

"Billy has it in his head that you stole Ireene's diamond engagement ring. He is telling pretty much everyone he encounters that you did."

Weird is an understatement for that, I think. "Seriously? Gram doesn't have a diamond engagement ring." Maybe that was a dumb thing to address first, but I have no idea what an appropriate response would be.

Sarah responds, "I didn't think she did. I was thinking maybe he remembers you showing us how you had his dad's ring reset and somehow in his brain that became you stealing your gram's ring."

Crimeny. Why can't things just be normal? Gram had

an engagement ring, of course. But it was set with a white sapphire. They couldn't afford a diamond in 1942 and they didn't know that white sapphire was soft and would scratch. When I was in high school, they told me that the ring would be mine one day. Pop wanted to know if I wanted them to reset it with a Cubic Zirconia so that it would look shiny and not dull and scratched. I told them no, that I didn't want a CZ. That the scratches all told stories from their life together and that is what I like about the ring, not whether it looks expensive or not. Gram gave me the ring awhile back, 2002 I think. Which Uncle Billy knew, of course. I wore it for several years, but then the stone tilted in the setting and I was afraid to wear it that the sapphire might fall out. *That* is the only engagement ring Gram ever had.

The ring I think Billy is talking about is the diamond that belonged to my grandfather. It was Great Grandma Hester's engagement ring. She gave it to my Pop when he was in his 20s. Her only requirement was that he not give the diamond to my grandmother, Ireene. Hester didn't like Ireene and didn't want her family diamond, what she called a Tiffany diamond, to go to Ireene (or at least that is the way Ireene has always told it).

So my grandfather had the ring set in a gold man's pinky ring with a small garnet on either side. He wore it every day of his life that I know of. When he died, the ring went to my father, who also wore it as a pinky ring. He wore it on days that he was not working on machinery in which it might get caught. When my father died, the ring went to me (Betty was to get a ring from my mom's side of the family). I wore it on a chain for awhile, but couldn't really wear it on my hand because it was sized as a man's pinky ring.

A couple of Thanksgivings ago, I asked Gram if it would be ok with her if, one day when I could afford it, I reset the diamond and garnets into a woman's ring, so that I could wear it. I was worried it would make her sad if I changed the shape of the ring so that it didn't look like Pop's and Dad's ring anymore. But she said, "Things are meant to be enjoyed, not saved in a drawer for someday." She thought making it wearable was a great idea. But, since it can be expensive to reset a ring, it stayed in my jewelry box until right after Gram went into the hospital. I was afraid she wouldn't live long, and I wanted her to see that I'd made the ring so that I could wear it. Michael and I talked about it and agreed to use our one and only credit card to pay to have the ring reset. Six hundred and fifty dollars later, I picked it up and it looked beautiful.

The first day I wore it to the nursing home to show Gram, the whole family happened to be there. I showed everyone and told her I'd gotten it reset so she could see me wear the family ring. She seemed happy, but was still pretty out of it at that point.

Uncle Billy's brain must have gotten the two rings confused and decided that I stole a diamond. I tell all this to Sarah. But honestly, I can't worry about what he believes, because it is taking all my energy to deal with everything for Gram. She is the one I promised to take care of, not him.

"I know you didn't, and I'm sorry. There are some things that Billy gets in his mind and they become real to him and there is no convincing him otherwise. But I wanted you to know before you heard it from someone else. And there's one other thing."

Then Sarah tells me that Gram's neighbor, Willa the medium, started visiting Gram this week and told Ireene that she doesn't have to listen to us, meaning Jay and I, and that Gram should do what she wants. Willa says she'll take care of Ireene when she gets home, or even that Ireene can come to live with her. That is interesting seeing as Willa hasn't visited Ireene once before this week, and since she only lives in the state a few months out of the year, I wonder who she thinks will take care of Ireene the rest of the time? I don't understand why Willa would tell Ireene "not to listen to us" even though

Willa has never talked to us to find out about Gram's medical situation.

Twenty-Five

Ireene

My granddaughter just left. GD. Granddaughter. GD. God Damn. That is what I started thinking while she was here. Granddaughter has the same two letters as God Damn. That is what I should call her from now on, because she is always in my God Damn business.

She and Jay are trying to force me to move to one of those expensive old people homes. Jay took me to see one, I think it was a few days ago. I liked it okay at first, and then I didn't. GD just brought me all these brochures about the places. I told her I can't afford it and that is all there is to it. She says there is a meeting set up in a few days with the facility staff to talk about the options for my leaving here. Says we need to talk about what is "safe" for me. Why wouldn't I be safe in my own home?

Billy says he'll come live with me and take care of me. If he did that, Sarah would have to come over at 5:30 each morning to give him his shots, because he can't do them himself. She would have to do one of those daily pill boxes for him too, because he doesn't know what medicine he takes. And Sarah would have to be sure to drive us both to our different doctors' appointments. Mars would have to stay with Sarah, since Billy can't see to take Mars for a walk outside. Yes, that just might work out.

Twenty-Six

The Granddaughter

I am about 45 minutes early for the meeting with the hospital staff. I just saw the Head Nurse on the way in and she stopped me. "Ireene is feeling particularly nasty today," she says. "She won't let anyone into her room to give her medicine and she snarls at anyone who tries. She is angry about this meeting today. Says we're all railroading her. You do understand that we'll have to let her go home if that is what she fights to do, right? We'll have the social worker there to try to dissuade her, but if she insists, then we'll have to shift into the mode of telling her what she needs to get set up for the house to be safer for her to live in, grip bars and stuff like that."

"Ok," I tell her, "We're going in now to tell her the idea we've come up with. We'll know by the time we come to the meeting if she'll do it."

Jay and I meet in the hall and go into Ireene's room together. Jay looks worried and I'm trying so hard to look happy when really I just want to throw up. The knots on the back of my neck make it feel like somebody pulled a slingshot back way too tight and it is fighting the force to let go.

I paste a smile on my face and say, "Hi Gram! Guess what? I'm kind of excited because I think I figured it out how you can afford to move to assisted living!" Smile stays in place.

Ireene says, " I told you I can't afford it."

"Well, just hear me out," I say. "I took your stock certificates to my friend that is the VP of an investment firm and he looked them up. Basically, you have about $50,000 in stocks. Isn't that great? It is way more than you thought you had. I also talked to a guy at the VA about a program that is for the surviving spouses of war veterans. That one will probably work later if you are low on money.

"But basically, you could live on the stock money and your income for a few months until the house sells. Then when the house sells, you can use that money and not use any more of the stocks.

"That way you are taking care of yourself with everything that is yours, but it makes it so you can live someplace safe where people can be around to help you if you need it."

"You went in my safe deposit box to get those certificates?" she asks, accusingly. I remind myself to breathe and remember that her brain doesn't function normally anymore and she can't help the way she reacts.

"Yes, Gram. We've talked about it a couple of times. You'd been telling me for weeks to go into the box and 'inventory' what was in there, and you were getting a little miffed at me because I hadn't yet. You knew it was a possibility that we might have to use them."

"But I told you I couldn't afford it."

"I know Gram, but like I said, I figured out a way for you to be able to afford it. And I honestly can't think of anything else to do."

"Fine," she says.

"Really?" I almost jumped off my chair.

"If that is what I have to do. But I don't want to. I want to go home."

I say, "Well, let's go to the meeting in a few minutes and we'll hear what the doctors suggest is best." Jay and I look at each other with just a little bit of hope starting to surface.

On the walk down, since she'd decided she didn't like Swiss Flowers, Jay and I tell her about a different Assisted Living Facility we found that looks awesome. Private rooms and Zen gardens. Even an area where she can start her own herb garden if she wants. She says yes, we can take her on a tour tomorrow.

Twenty-Seven

The Granddaughter

We all get situated in a conference room. Grandma to my right, Billy next to her, Billy's wife behind him, Jay and the nurse, the Occupational Therapy person, and social worker on the other sides of the table.

Grandma sits quietly in her wheelchair. The Head Nurse starts off - because Ireene is on blood thinners and has very thin skin, and she is very unsteady walking, that creates the risk that she will fall and get cut and then bleed out. She says that she's talked to the staff and the doctor and they all agree that some type of Assisted Living Facility would be the best choice so that Ireene doesn't end up falling with no one around to find and help her. That way Ireene could be sure of having nutritious meals and someone to help her keep track of her medicines.

Ireene's face grows instantly dark, "I know what medicines I'm taking now," she booms. She looks at the OT lady and says, "She makes me take a test every day to see if I can remember them well enough to do them when I'm at home. And I pass. I've been doing my own medicine for years at home, I shouldn't have to prove to you now that I can do it. Tell them I passed!"

OT lady flinches a little and says, "Oh she did! Ireene does wonderfully in OT. And I talked to her physical therapist and he says she is walking well with a walker too."

Ireene seizes the opportunity and says, "They both agree I can go home! You heard her."

Head Nurse nods and says evenly, "Yes, it does sound like you are doing very well in those areas. I don't doubt that at all. But regardless of those things, we feel that your health status alone warrants you living at some type of monitored facility."

"Well I can't afford that," she spits out. Then at me, "Don't you sit over there and smile. Do you think I can't see you smirking like I'm a fool? Is something funny about this?" The room grows still and I can tell social worker is surprised at the outburst.

"Gram, I'm only smiling because I knew you were going to say you can't afford it because that is what you always say. But we just talked about it in your room and I showed you how you can afford it. If money was the ultimate reason you said you couldn't go, we've fixed that problem."

"That was before she said I could go home!" she jabs a finger in the direction of the OT lady. If I could give the OT lady a slap in the back of the head, I think I would at this moment.

The Head Nurse chimes in, "I don't think what Karen was saying is that you should go home and live by yourself, but that you are coming along very well at healing and getting your memory back. But since there are still big lapses in memory and the other physical things we mentioned, it still isn't the best option for you to live alone. Please remember that OT and Physical Therapy alone do not determine your course of action," she says, eyeing the OT lady, "Your whole medical team together gives its recommendation.

"Now if you insist on it, on going home, we'll need to talk about some things that you'll have to do to your house to make it safer for you when you get home. An example of the things I mean are handrails..."

Ireene interrupts her, "I don't use the handrails here anymore and I don't need them. So I'm not paying to have them in my house if I won't use them."

Head Nurse continues on as though there were no interruption, "...and a toilet booster seat to make the distance less that you have to sit down, which makes for less chance of a fall."

Ireene jumps in again, her face twisting in anger, "I WILL NOT USE A BOOSTER SEAT on the toilet. That is outrageous and it is just foolish to make me buy one when I don't need it!" Her voice is raised and she sounds frantic, "I am not a child!"

Then Ireene says, "I have to go home and do my shredding."

Obviously perplexed, the Head Nurse repeats, "Your shredding?"

"I have 30 years of tax returns that I have to shred. I can't move until I shred all those papers and it takes a long time to do. I've only done the first five years so far."

I'm sitting here just trying to breathe calmly and keep a composed look on my face. The conversation goes around a few more times, mentions are made of Meals on Wheels and Life Alert, and it eventually becomes obvious that we've hit an impasse. Ireene refuses to talk any more. Her agitation and yelling in this meeting seem to have convinced the staff even more that their recommendation for supervised living was correct. The Head Nurse points out that Ireene's insistence that she will not do any of the things that the medical team recommends somewhat proves the fact that she is not capable of making reasonable decisions about her own care. But they know they cannot force the issue as long as she is still "competent". I'm wondering what the heck she'd have to do to be considered incompetent.

I say, "Well, we have two more days before Ireene has to be out of the room here. Let us talk privately about it some more and we'll try to let you know tomorrow and we can make plans from there."

The hospital staff nod and agree. Everyone stands up and shakes hands, Ireene is already shuffling her feet trying to push back from the table and head towards the door. Billy tries to help her, but he can't see where he is going when he pushes her, so they can't get out the door. The OT lady helps them get out the door and Billy drives Gram to her room.

I walk outside with Jay and Sarah. I tell them, feeling

totally defeated, "Well, that was ugly. I don't know about you guys, but I don't want to think about this anymore today."

Twenty-Eight

The Granddaughter

Gram called tonight. I guess she figured trying to hear on the phone was worth it at this point. She opened with, "You didn't tell me what time you are picking me up tomorrow." Seriously? I have the urge to jump off of something very high.

"Gram, after the meeting today, it seemed like you decided you are moving home on your own." I can hear my patience sounding strained.

She replies, "I told you I'd go see it and I'll go see it."

We arrange for Jay and I to pick her up at 9 am and we say goodnight. This is not a fun rollercoaster.

I decide to spend the evening curled up with my husband watching a movie and not thinking about all of this. Too many nights lately have been taken up with paperwork and medical reports. We get settled on the couch and my tiny little old dog walks into the room. She is 15 years old and has canine Lupus. She is getting a bit old and confused and sometimes just wanders around the house. She gives us the onceover and turns around and goes back to her bed. I'm struck by how similar my dog and my grandmother can be sometimes.

I lay my head back on my husband's chest and try to get myself ready for another crazy day tomorrow.

Twenty-Nine

Aunt Jay

Lorna and I just dropped Ireene back off at the nursing home after taking her on a tour of Sea Breeze. True to Ireene form, she was relatively good during the tour and then had a fit afterwards. The Business Manager at Sea Breeze is a very good looking man named Chad.

Ireene has always been partial to good looking people. She is very proud of the fact that she was beautiful when she was young and that Henry was handsome. On a regular basis she comments on how good looking her children are and were. And she has been known to show less than a little tact when telling other people how she feels about their appearances. I remember once she gave my niece a bread maker as a gift. When my niece opened it, she was excited about it and started talking about what types of bread she'd be able to make for her family. Ireene's response to this was, "Well, you better not make it too often or you'll get fat, and no husband wants a fat wife."

Ireene just loved Business Manager Chad. She was nicer to him than she's been to anyone in weeks. He showed her the private rooms that are like little apartments. To him she said it looks wonderful. To us she said I can't afford it. He showed her the dining room with a private area in case she wanted to have the family for dinner. To him she said, oh yes, that would be nice. To us she says, I can't afford it and I'm not going to pay them to make food I'm not going to eat. He showed her the walking paths, party gathering area, and gardens. To him she said, I do like to garden. To us she says, I still can't afford it.

What's interesting is that she has never once asked how much it costs. Her concept of money has been really off since November. Things she would usually spend $5 on, because she has budgeted so carefully, she thinks she should spend $100 on now. She doesn't seem to connect how much she has or how much things should cost. Lorna has been doing her bills for months, and at first Ireene seemed interested in staying involved, but by now she just seems to take it for granted that everything is getting done. As many times as she has said she can't afford Assisted Living, I honestly don't think she has a concept of what that means.

It was in the car on the way back to the nursing home that things exploded. Ireene says she doesn't care how many places we take her or how good they look, she can't afford it and we can't change that. She says she wants to go home and we're holding her hostage and making her do something she doesn't want to do. That we purposely made her house unlivable so she wouldn't be able to go back there. Billy has been big on this lately too. He was with us when we started packing up Ireene's house, but now he says that he disagreed with it the whole time. He tells Ireene and Sarah and Ireene's neighbors that Lorna and I are unreasonable and are trying to take Ireene's things for ourselves.

Lorna is driving and Ireene is in the front seat; I'm squished in the back seat with Ireene's walker. I can see Lorna's face in the rear view mirror and it looks like she is doing some deep breathing. I've noticed over the last few months that when Lorna is trying to keep calm and not say what she is thinking, she takes a couple deep breaths and rolls her head and shoulders like she is trying to remove a kink. She is doing that now, so I know she must be trying hard not to respond to Ireene's accusations. She tries once again to explain to Ireene that the doctors think it is best that she not live at home alone.

It takes about fifteen minutes to get from Sea Breeze back to the nursing home and Ireene uses that time to berate Lorna on a number of topics. Last month, my husband John started cleaning Ireene's pool once a week so that Lorna could cancel the pool service and save Ireene $75 a month. Lorna made the mistake of mentioning that to Ireene and she has been on a warpath ever since. Lorna had no right to cancel her pool service, and because Lorna did, the pool would get ruined and need to be resurfaced for $15,000 and Ireene doesn't have $15,000. No one can quite figure out where that one is coming from. She wants to know did Lorna cancel the lawn service to ruin her lawn too? So many conversations go like that lately. It is amazing that Ireene cannot remember most things from day to day, but there are a few things that she remembers and cannot let go. The more she worries over them, the more paranoid and angry she gets.

When we got back to the facility, we got Ireene back into her room. Tomorrow is moving day, and we still haven't locked this down. That is when Lorna said, "Look Gram, you can't stay here and you've got to go somewhere. You clearly have decided what you want to do, regardless of what the doctors say. And you are going to keep thinking that Jay and I are doing you wrong, regardless of the fact that everything we've done for months is with your best interest in mind. And Jay and I are not, as you say, going to "hold you hostage". So you win. I will bring you the box with your checkbook and your bills that I've paid and your credit cards. You'll need to have your phone turned back on in your house. Tomorrow you'll be able to sign your discharge papers and head home. You'll need to call Sea Breeze and tell them you're not coming. I'm sorry you've been so unhappy with me and with the way I've been trying to keep things going for you. I love you, but I need to go now."

I wasn't expecting that! I mean, Lorna and I have been talking about the possibility of course. The nursing home says Ireene can legally make her own decisions. Ireene wants to go home. Billy thinks Lorna is a thief who is using this situation as a way to manically control Ireene's life and take her belongings. And Ireene's neighbors think Lorna is trying to force Ireene to move so that she can take whatever she wants from Ireene's house and her bank account. They think Ireene will do just fine at home and say they'll keep an eye out for her.

So I knew that it was a possibility that she would end up going home, I just wasn't expecting Lorna to say that this afternoon. Ireene looks triumphant; Lorna looks defeated. Lorna and I walk to the parking lot together. We talk for a few minutes and agree that we're making ourselves crazy trying to do the right thing when for some reason the people immediately around Ireene don't think we are. Which is interesting, because every step of the way the last few months, Lorna has sent detailed updates to all members of the family, asking for input, suggestions, and agreement. Every single decision that has been made, she ran by the family first. I remember her saying one day that she didn't think it was reasonable for her to make decisions about Ireene on her own. She wanted to make sure everyone was in agreement. The members of the family who do not have brain trauma are still completely on board with what Lorna has been trying to do. Billy and Ireene, not so much. And the neighbors, who knows what they are thinking? They haven't been involved in all the caretaking and meetings and paperwork, but they feel like they still have every clue what is best for Ireene.

I get in my car and start to pull out of the parking lot. As I pass Lorna's car, I can see her sitting with her head in her hands.

Thirty

The Granddaughter

I got home and told Michael everything that happened. He said, "Good, Honey. You've been making yourself sick for weeks with this. At some point you just have to let go and realize you can't fix it." I just feel so awful, my head is pounding and my chest is tight. I promised, when I signed Gram's paperwork a few years back, to do what is necessary to make sure she is medically and financially taken care of should she not be able to deal directly with those things herself. The doctors say she shouldn't go home, but they say it is her choice. I can't keep fighting trying to do what is best for her when she is legally able to do what she wants, even if what she wants is contradictory to what her doctors say is best.

My phone rings and I see the nursing home's number on the caller ID. What now? I steel myself and answer the phone.

Ireene cuts right to the chase, "I need you to come sign all my paperwork in the morning." I guess she is over her phase of not wanting to talk on the phone.

"No you don't," I respond. "You are legally able to sign for yourself and you don't need me to do it."

"But I need you to sign me in at Sea Breeze," she says.

"No, you don't. You can sign that contract too. But you said you weren't going there anyway."

"I *have* to go," she responds. "You set it up so I have to go. So now you need to do the paperwork. They won't let me since you've done everything."

"Gram, you don't *have* to go. We didn't sign a contract yet. But if going there is what you are deciding to do, I'll drop your checkbook off to you early in the a.m., so you can pay your deposit when you check in."

"I have to move there because you told them I would."

"No, you don't. I'm not going to let you blame this move on me too. You've been blaming everything on me for months, and I'm not willing to accept blame anymore. This is all your choice. If you move home, it is your choice. If you move to Sea Breeze, it is your choice." I can hear my voice getting louder and I hate that I'm getting upset. Arguing with a woman who has brain damage just doesn't make sense, but I can't help it.

Ireene says, "If I go home, will you keep paying my bills and doing my paperwork for me?"

"No," I say. "The doctors say you should live in Assisted Living in order to be healthy and safe. That is what I'm willing to help you do. If you choose to go home where you could fall and bleed to death, that is up to you. But if you feel that you are stable enough to move home on your own, then you need to be able to do your bills on your own too."

"I need you to keep doing them. You said I have to move to Sea Breeze, so I will," she responds.

"Gram, move to Sea Breeze if you want, but don't put that decision off on me."

"Billy said you tried to have my driver's license taken away," Ireene spits out.

"What?" I respond. What the hell? Why does this have to come up now? Technically, I did look into having her license taken away. Our state has a "Grand-Drivers" program where anyone can report the plate number of an aged driver to the state, who will then send an investigator to evaluate whether the person should continue driving. If the state would just stop letting ninety-year-olds renew their driver's licenses by mail for six years, they probably wouldn't need the Grand-Drivers program. At any rate, after Gram told me last year that she can't feel her feet up to her knees, I emailed the family asking what they thought and whether we should consider contacting the Grand-Driver's program. Most of the family agreed, but Sarah seemed distressed as that would likely mean that she'd have to drive Ireene around in addition to Billy. So at that point, I didn't take it any further. I tried talking to Ireene about using Senior Rides, but she just said her usual, "I can't afford it." No matter how I pointed out that without having to pay insurance on her car, she could afford it easily, she wouldn't budge.

Ireene now repeats, "Billy said you tried to take my driver's license away."

I just don't feel like talking anymore, "Gram, you and I talked about using Senior Rides last year and you wouldn't do it." I don't try defending the fact that I didn't actually turn her in to that program. That sort of seems like it would be splitting hairs.

"I need you to pick me up and take me to Sea Breeze in the morning," she says. Oh, now I get where she was going with the driver's license thing.

"Gram, honestly I'm at the point where I can't really talk to you right now. I've been doing my best and all I get back from you is accusations. And I just don't want to keep putting myself in that position. If you are really going to Sea Breeze, I'll go early in the morning and fill out all the paperwork if that is what you want. I won't sign it though, you'll have to sign for yourself, so later when you say I made you go there, you can look back and see your own signature on the contract.

"I'll get someone to pick you up and take you over there. But for tomorrow at least, it won't be me," I finish.

"You need to do my exit paperwork here."

My patience is very close to snapping completely, so I say, "Fine, I'll go down in the morning, sign your paperwork there, then go to Sea Breeze and fill out that paperwork. I'll ask Jay or someone to pick you up at 10 am and bring you over to Sea Breeze. All you'll have to do is sign the contract and you can move in."

"But it has to be you!"

"Gram, no it doesn't. I'll set everything up and

someone will help you tomorrow. But I don't think it is good for either one of us to be together right now. Goodnight, Gram." And I hung up.

I'm crying yet again and Michael comes into the room and puts his arms around me. "I'm proud of you," he says. "You did the right thing."

Thirty-One

The Granddaughter

Something Gram said the other day is niggling at me. "Willa said she'll take care of me." I remember Gram telling me once that a lady "gave" Willa a lot of money. I didn't really question it at the time, but now I'm starting to wonder.

I flip open our laptop on the dining room table. I have boxes of Gram's paperwork hogging the rest of the table. It is a good thing we eat in the living room most of the time! I open Google and search on "Willa Jones". I get one hit on an interview with Willa on the Today Show. The host asks her what she says to critics who suggest she is a phony. Her response? "Not everyone understands what I do." The next hit I get is a bit alarming, "Psychic Steals Estate of Dying Woman, Family Sues". It is a long article that boils down to Willa befriending a woman in hospice who was dying of Parkinson's Disease. Within one month of meeting Willa, and just two days before she died, the woman changed her will and signed over her estate worth over a million dollars to Willa.

Oh yes, this is the woman I want "taking care of" my grandmother. Especially since Willa has already told Gram once that she wants Gram's house. It strikes me that Willa didn't say she wants to buy Gram's house, just that she "wants" it.

This is a serious problem. I hit the print button, then call my sister, Betty, to fill her in.

Thirty-Two

Ireene

It takes me a little longer to get dressed these days, so I start early. I have to be ready by 10 am for Lorna to pick me up to take me to the new place. I put on my thick sweater, because it is always cold in here.

Jay and John walk in and I say, "What are you doing here? I'm moving today, I can't visit with you."

Jay says, "We know, Ireene, we're here to help you pack your things and to take you over to Sea Breeze. Lorna told you last night that we would come pick you up."

"No she didn't. She said she would come pick me up. She has to sign me in over there."

It is John that answers, "No she doesn't. She filled out all your paperwork over there this morning. All you have to do is sign on the dotted line, write them a check, and move your stuff in." This is just all so confusing. First she says I have to move, then she doesn't show up to help me.

I watch Jay and John put my things into boxes. They make a couple of trips to the car, then say we're ready to go. Someone in white comes in and says I have to sign a paper. I don't know what the paper is, but I sit down and try to focus on finding the line I'm supposed to sign on.

We're in the car on the way when I say, "I think my granddaughter just doesn't want me to see what she's taken from my house. That's why she won't let me move back there."

John replies, "Ireene, you've known Lorna her whole life. Do you really think she would steal from you? Why would you have appointed her to do all of your legal and medical things if you didn't trust her?"

"I didn't have anyone else; I had to have her do it. But that was before, now she's taken over and won't let me do things on my own. She's too pushy about everything."

"Ireene, you can't do things on your own. You are so convinced you can go live by yourself, but you've had someone helping you do everything since the day you fell. But who is going to help you with them at home? You keep saying your neighbors or Sarah will come by, someone will do your bills, someone will take you to the doctor, someone will take you to go shopping. Why are you willing to have so many people alter their lives just because you are being stubborn? But you aren't willing to do a single thing like put up hand rails or use Meals on Wheels. You're the one making this difficult, not Lorna." John said.

I don't want to hear him anymore, so I turn my hearing aids down until we arrive at Sea Breeze.

Thirty-Three

Ireene

I think I need to start trying to hold my tongue when my granddaughter is around. She is coming to pick me up to take me to my house and to get some things at the store to stock my new apartment at this place. She sounds like she is going to stop taking care of things for me, so I need her to calm down.

This room is nice looking, but the shower gets water on the floor. I can't bend down to mop it up with a towel. How am I supposed to take a shower if it gets water on the floor?

I have my own key to my apartment. I don't know who else has one, maybe my granddaughter and Billy? I couldn't sleep at all last night; someone kept coming into my room and looking at me.

Thirty-Four

The Granddaughter

Wow. Today actually went really well. Gram and I spent the entire day together. First we went to her house and she surveyed everything we'd done while she was gone. She looked at the boxes and asked me a few questions. She took a few things to hang at her new place, and a ceramic eagle and a shelf to sit it on. I'm sure it was hard for her to see her house like that, but she handled it well. At one point she even said, "See, I'm being nice." That was an odd statement. It leads me to believe that she *does* know what a mean beast she's been. I liked it better when I thought she wasn't in control of how mean she was being. A couple of her neighbors stopped by to see her because they saw my car in the driveway. They looked at me like I was the enemy.

Because Gram mentions daily that she could go live at home and Willa would take of her, I brought the printout of the article I read on Willa and showed it to Gram. "Gram, I just thought you should know what information is out there about Willa before you give her too much rein in your life."

Ireene looks at it and responds, "My friend isn't like that." And that was the end of the conversation.

We grabbed a few plants to put on her new patio. I found a 12-inch flag on a stick and asked if she wanted to bring it so she could have a flag at her new place too. She liked that idea.

After her house we went to the pharmacy to pick up prescriptions. I handed her a credit card and she paid for them. It seemed to make her happy to do something that felt "normal". Then she said, "I need you to take me to pick up some wine." The look she gave me was like, "I dare you to say no." I sighed and figured that she's lived this long drinking like she does, Sea Breeze said alcohol isn't encouraged, but it isn't prohibited, and she feels like everything else is being taken away from her, so if a bottle of wine makes her happy, so be it. It turned out to be three bottles of wine, but who's counting?

Then to the grocery store for "snacks". Shopping takes a really long time when you are with a 96-year-old woman who can only shuffle a couple of inches at a time. But she seemed happy to be out, so I went with it. Our outing took the entire day and I couldn't believe she had the energy for it all. Maybe she is doing better than I thought.

When we got back to Sea Breeze, she insisted on carrying armloads of stuff to her room. I tried to carry most of it and she got snippy that she would carry it herself. The only problem with that is that it made her even more unstable. So as she tripped on a crack in the sidewalk, I grabbed her and righted her before she went down. Then she just kept on walking like nothing happened. As she passed her new neighbors on her way to her apartment, she said, " I have wine for happy hour!"

I called maintenance to ask them to come hang her shelf for her. And she wanted to hang my painting in the hallway. They said they'd probably get there tomorrow. As I was leaving, Ireene says, "I made it all day being nice, didn't I?"

She'd been really upset about not having her credit cards. We agreed that since she didn't have cash or her checkbook, that I would leave her a credit card and department store card. That way if one of her friends came to take her to lunch, she could pay for her own. That seemed to make her happy. She put the two cards in her otherwise empty wallet and put it on her nightstand.

There was no phone in the room, so I brought Ireene's hearing disabled phone with large buttons and really loud volume over from her house. I didn't bring the answering machine, because she never could get it to work anyway. She'd always say, "Everything comes out garbled." But when

I'd listen to it, it would sound fine. I didn't really want to say, "No, it is your hearing that is garbled."

I plug the phone in and test it to make sure it is in working order. I hand her the address book that she has stuffed to the gills with numbers for everyone she has met in the last 50 years.

I stopped at the office on the way out to check with them to be sure they have the emergency contact info correct in case they need to get a hold of me. They said since Ireene insisted on choosing the package that allows her to administer her own medicines, that they would simply ask her every day if she took them, but could not touch them or offer to help her, since the pills did not come through their pharmacy.

Part of Ireene's discharge plan from the nursing home is that she will be visited twice per week by a visiting nurse for the first four weeks she is in Assisted Living. After that it will be once per month. She is to continue to regularly see her own doctors.

Thirty-Five

Aunt Jay

I have laundry detergent with me, because Ireene wants to go to the laundry room at her new place to learn how to use the machines so she can do her own laundry. It is on the other side of the facility, and I'm not sure how she is going to get her laundry there, but it is another one of those things that it is just easier to go with.

I look at the counter in her kitchenette and see that the prescription bottles Lorna picked up yesterday with Ireene are still in the pharmacy bags. "Aunt Ireene, did you take your pills last night and this morning?"

"Yes," Ireene responds.

"But they are all still sealed up in the bags from the pharmacy," I say.

"I TOOK THEM!" is Ireene's reply. Then she says, "My TV doesn't work."

"I don't know if they've hooked up the cable yet. I thought you didn't want cable since you never watch TV."

"I want the TV to work. I'm paying to have it in the room, it should work," she says, eyeballing the flat screen TV hanging on the wall. I make a mental note to ask Lorna about cable.

Later in the afternoon, when I've been home for about an hour, I get a call from Ireene. She is frantic that she lost her credit cards and can't find them. She needs me to come back over right now and help her look, because she's looked everywhere and doesn't want Lorna to know that she lost them.

Soooo, I get back in the car and head back to Ireene's place. She hasn't left, as far as I know, since I was there this afternoon, so they can't have gone too far. When I get there she is beside herself and has every drawer and cabinet open.

She is holding a towel on her head where she walked into one of the open cabinets and cut her head. I have her sit down so I can put a bandage on her head. Then I start looking for the cards. After 15 minutes, I finally find them in the toe of a shoe in her closet. She looks at the shoe blankly and says, "I must have put them there for safe keeping."

Thirty-Six

The Granddaughter

At the end of Ireene's first week at Sea Breeze, I get a call from Marge, the manager of the visiting nurse company. She says that Ireene's blood thinner levels are dangerously low and if they don't get righted, she'll be back in the hospital within days.

I call Sea Breeze and switch her plan from the self-administration of medications to facility- administration. Then we have to reorder all the medications through their pharmacy. That is $400 more even after Medicare and coinsurance.

I call Sarah and ask her to please take Ireene's medications from her room when she visits today. Since I'm an hour away, I go down twice a week now, but Sarah still takes Uncle Billy and the dog every day. I don't envy Sarah telling Ireene she won't be administering her own pills anymore. But I'm guessing the threat of going back to the hospital will be enough.

Gram calls me tonight to tell me that her TV still doesn't work. She doesn't mention the medicine, just the TV. I had cable connected, so I tell her I'll check with Sea Breeze and hopefully they can send someone to her room tomorrow. She is pissed, because it hasn't worked since she moved in and wants to know why she's paying for it if it doesn't work.

Thirty-Seven

Ireene

Someone stole my phone. They replaced it with a big-buttoned phone last night when they thought I was asleep. I can't sleep with people coming in and out all night, so I was awake when someone snuck in and took my phone and replaced it with this one.

I sit in the chair by my front door waiting for Jay to come. I can't turn the TV on because it doesn't work. I can't talk on the phone, because it isn't my phone. I don't want to go out into the garden, because there is a crazy lady that talks to everyone when they step out of their rooms. So I just sit and look at the door until Jay knocks on it.

As soon as Jay walks in I say, "Someone stole my phone!"

She looks around the room and says, "Aunt Ireene, your phone is right there on the floor next to the table."

"That isn't my phone, someone switched that one out with my phone last night when they thought I was asleep," I say. Jay crosses the room and picks up the phone.

Looking at it she says, "Aunt Ireene, this IS your phone. Lorna brought it from your house for you."

"THAT is a big-buttoned phone!" I say.

Jay looks at me like I'm a fool and says, "Your phone is a big-buttoned phone. This is the same one. Ivory. Extra loud volume."

"DON'T LIE TO ME!" I yell at her. "You are always LYING to me! I need you to go to my house and bring back the right phone."

"Aunt Ireene, I don't know what to tell you. I don't know how to make this better for you, because this is your phone. And honestly, even if it weren't, it still works, right?"

"It. Is. Not. My. Phone." I don't want to talk to her

anymore and I tell her so. She looks around the room, then leaves quietly out the door.

I need to go to my house and get my shredder. I need to shred my back taxes.

I pick up the phone, squint, and dial my granddaughter's phone number. I get one of those phone message things that I hate. When it beeps I say, "I hate these damn machines! Don't you ever answer your damn phone? Someone stole my phone and I want the one from my house back. And I need my shredder."

Thirty-Eight

The Granddaughter

Ugh, I think as I dial Gram's number to return her call. Her message was just so sweet I can't wait to talk to her. "Hi Gram. I got your message, are you doing ok?"

"Jay is lying to me."

"What do you mean, Gram. Why would Jay lie to you?" I ask.

"Someone switched my phone for another one and she is trying to convince me they didn't. Maybe it was even her that did it."

"Gram, why would anyone switch your phone? If you look at it, you can see that it is the same one that I brought over from your house."

"It is NOT! You'll see when you come here. It is someone else's phone," she says.

"Ok, Gram. I'll check it out next time I come down. How about the TV, does it work now?"

" Yes, they came and now it works. I am not a big TV watcher though, so it doesn't really do me any good," she states.

Ireene hesitates then says, "I know I'm being obnoxious, but I have to be."

"Why do you feel you have to be, Gram?"

"I just do," she says.

I get off the phone with Ireene, grab a soda, and sit on the couch to check my email, only to find a nasty-gram from Uncle Billy ranting about something that just makes no sense whatsoever. I get that he is mad, but for the life I me I can't figure out at what. I'm certainly not going to go out of my way to ask. Delete button for that one. Then there is one from the manager at Sea Breeze telling me that Ireene attempted to hit the aide last night that was trying to give her pills. The manager says they won't be able to put their staff in jeopardy to give her medication, so she is hoping it doesn't happen again. I'm not really sure how to control that.

Later that night when I'm talking to Jay, she says, "Ireene told me the other day that Willa took her shopping for shoes and Ireene bought a pair that was $75 at a boutique."

"No she didn't!" I say, "Ireene has never spent more than $15 on a pair of shoes in her life. She wears her gardening shoes and her church shoes. There is no way that she'd spend $75 on shoes."

"Well, she says she did," say Jay. "She said Willa told her that she just had to have them! Of course, I guess it could just be because Ireene was just confused. She said when she got them home she decided they weren't comfortable and stowed them away in a box in her closet." I'll have to check the credit card bill when it comes. I write myself a reminder to have the limits lowered on Ireene's credit cards, so that it isn't possible for her to run up a bill.

We compare notes about the mystery of the stolen phone, trying to at least find some humor in the situation.

Thirty-Nine

Aunt Jay

When I stopped by to see Aunt Ireene today, she asked me if I remembered her telling me she didn't want to see me anymore? I told her I knew she was upset when we were talking about the phone, but I wasn't mad about it. She says no, what she means is, she doesn't want me to visit. Ouch.

But then Ireene calls this afternoon and asks, "Don't I have a doctor's appointment tomorrow? I have one written on my calendar."

"Yes, you are supposed to see your regular doctor tomorrow."

"Are you going to take me?" she asks. Oh boy. John would tell me to count to ten.

Forty

Ireene

I'm waiting for my doctor to come in and am thinking I want to bring more of my things to this place they are making me live so that nothing else disappears from my house. Who knows what kinds of things they've taken by now. Dr. Snow walks in and asks, "And how are we today, Ireene?"

"Pretty unhappy if you want to know," I say.

"Really? Why is that?" Dr. Snow asks.

"They forced me to move to a place I don't want to be. Those people are making me take pills that are too big for me to swallow. And they won't let me go for a walk."

Jay jumps in, "Aunt Ireene, you can walk as much as you want on the trails and in the gardens."

"I don't want to walk on the trails! I want to walk on the road. I want to walk to the grocery store."

Dr. Snow says, "To the grocery store? I thought your Assisted Living was on the key? There aren't any grocery stores on the key."

"I don't care!" I reply. "I want to go for a walk and I want to decide where I do it."

Dr. Snow says, "You understand, don't you, that it would be a legal liability for the facility to allow someone who is a fall risk to leave on their own, on foot, with nothing around to walk to?"

"I don't care about them. I don't like them, especially that manager lady. I don't want to live there."

"Where do you want to be?"

"My own house!" I say.

"Do you think you manage there on your own?" Dr. Snow asks.

"Well, I may not be able to do everything the way I used to," I concede.

"So what is the answer? What will make you happy?

"To die," I say, glaring at her.

Dr. Snow narrows her eyes at me like she is trying to decide if I mean it. She says, "Well, Ireene, if that is truly what you want, then you can simply stop taking this top medication on your list. If you keep taking it, you'll probably live to be 100. But if you'd prefer, I can stop prescribing it for you. Maybe you've done all the living you wanted to do."

What the hell kind of answer is that for a doctor? "I'll keep taking them," I say. "But I won't like it."

I get up and grab my cane and start walking out of the office. I keep walking right past the reception desk and outside. Jay can catch up with me if she wants to.

Forty-One

The Granddaughter

I am sitting at work and have a feeling like there is an elephant sitting on my chest. Wow, it feels like I'm having a heart attack. Ok, dial it back a notch, I think. It isn't a heart attack. What is it that people are usually having when they think they are having a heart attack? An anxiety attack. Great. I'm truly starting to fall apart. I keep pressing my fist into my breast bone to try to relieve the pressure.

Michael is worried about me. He knows I'm not sleeping most nights and he worries that I'm making myself sick. He can't stand hearing that Billy and Ireene are accusing me of things after I've spent all this time trying to take care of Ireene. We both know they are being irrational and paranoid, but that doesn't make it hurt any less. He says we have to do something, because I'm crying more and more often. I was happy before, and now the happiness doesn't seem to have any room to stay with all the negative things fighting for my attention.

We try to come up with alternatives, but nothing presents itself. I'm starting to dread the sound of my phone ringing. I've changed my ring tone twice to see if I can find one that doesn't make my blood pressure spike automatically. I've never talked on the phone this much in my life; I've even had to up the minutes on my cell plan.

I got one of Uncle Billy's crazy emails today. He'll go for a couple of days with none, then some days he sends four or five, sometimes about the same thing, because he forgets he sent the earlier ones. Uncle Billy was always a bit on the existential side, so the way he talked and wrote was always a little out there. But since his accident, some of his emails sound like the March Hare meets the Grateful Dead's Dancing Bears, they drop some acid, and then sit down to compose an email. This one was no exception.

"L, checked the jewelry box again. Still empty. Great. Am I kvetching? Did you know I can speak Yiddish when cornered? Another talent the aliens let stay in my head. You spelled Coumadin wrong in your last email. You are a jackass if you think I'm going to help you blindside Ireene. Love, B"

Yeah, love you too, Uncle Billy.

Forty-Two

The Granddaughter

Aunt Jay warned me that Gram was on a new tear, but I didn't realize the level of bile we were talking about. I was eating dinner tonight when my phone rang. Blood pressure spike? Check. I answer and hear Ireene on the other end of the line.

"Hi Gram."

"Why would you do it?" Ireene says.

"Why would I do what?" I say, knowing what she is going to say, because of Jay's warning, and thinking that this is going to be even worse than when she said Jay, John, and I hired an incompetent home appraiser to do a report on her house. He didn't, she said, know how to calculate the square footage of her house, and she is not going to sell her house based on calculations from a man who doesn't know what he is doing. And it wasn't our business anyway to have her house appraised, because she couldn't sell it until her shredding was complete. I pointed out that if she shreds one year of paperwork per week, it will take months for her to finish, and that her finances cannot support her to live in Assisted Living *and* pay for her house to be empty for months. She called me about that appraisal every day for a week before she moved onto something else.

Now she is saying, "Why would you saw my grandfather clock in half?" I almost laugh because the absurdity of that question is too much.

I sigh, "What are you talking about, Gram?"

"Billy told me that you and Jay said you are going to saw the grandfather clock into pieces and take it from my house!"

"Why would we do that Gram?"

"I don't know! Why would you? You CANNOT cut the

clock that has been in my family since the 1800s!" she screeches.

"Gram, that doesn't make any sense. Jay and I have no reason to saw your furniture. Are you sure that is what Uncle Billy told you? Maybe you misunderstood him."

"I did not. I told him that I wanted to get some more things from my house and bring them here to my apartment."

"You're not going to have room for too much more in there Gram. You keep having Sarah move stuff over; you won't be able to fit a whole house of stuff into a two room apartment," I say.

"I'm not trying to fit the whole house, I just WANT WHAT'S MINE!"

I remain silent because there doesn't seem to be a good response to that.

"I have to take these things," she yells, "so you and Jay can't take everything from my house and saw my grandfather clock in half!"

I can't help it, I say, "What part of that sounds reasonable to you?" I notice Michael going around and closing windows, so I guess I might be yelling a little bit too. "Have you been to the house lately? EVERYTHING is still there in the boxes on the floor exactly as it was the first time I took you there after you moved! Everything that is except what you've taken to your apartment."

"You sound hysterical," Ireene says.

"I SOUND HYSTERICAL? Are you kidding me? You have truly lost it. You think I am sawing your furniture in half, but I'm the one who sounds hysterical? Gram, you are honestly making me crazy. There is nothing I can do to make you happy. Even when I think you are doing okay, I find out that you've been saying awful things about me to other people. Did you think I didn't know that you're only nice to my face so I'll keep doing all your grunt work for you? To listen to you and Uncle Billy, you'd think I was an axe murderer. Oh wait, apparently I'm a grandfather clock murderer."

"Well, I just don't know why you would do it. So I had to call and ask you. I had to."

I say, "Gram, I don't know if I can help you anymore. No matter what I try, you are miserable and you are making me miserable. I need to think about this. I'll talk to you later."

Part II

Forty-Three

Lorna

I've talked to my sister, my mother, aunts, uncles (except Uncle Billy, of course), and cousins to share with them what I plan to do and each agrees it will be for the best.

Several times over the last five months or so, I've called and talked to Gram's estate attorney. I kept him up on what was happening with Ireene and asked his advice in certain areas. For example, I gave him the information about what the doctors suggested for Gram's living arrangements and also about Gram's wishes, and asked him if I was, in his opinion, doing the right thing in trying to get her to move to Assisted Living. Another area I'd asked him about was if the occasion were to arise where Gram was to have someone convince her to give her house to or change her will to include that person, would this be allowed given Gram's state of mind and health? He was helpful on both counts and said that he thought it was much better to research the possibility of elder exploitation than to have to figure out what to do once it has happened.

This week I visited him in person, with Jay, for the first time (again, thinking it is always better to have two people hear something than just one). I'd never met him in person. He looked a little wary at first given that Gram is his client, not me, as he squeezed us into the smallest conference room I've ever seen. I got the distinct idea its purpose was to dissuade long conversations. But once he realized what I wanted, he was much more open. Yes, he said, it is very reasonable to have a professional guardian appointed for Ireene, and given everything I've told him, he can see where it would be in her best interest. He gave us the name of another lawyer in town who specializes in Elder Law.

Since I took the day off of work to spend the day in Gram's town researching this, I figured I'd better at least attempt to see the lawyer in person today, so that I didn't have to take off another day to come back and see him. So Jay and I went and camped out in his lobby until he became available. We sat drinking coffee and talking in low voices about what our possible options were. We clinked coffee cups and toasted ourselves a Happy Valentine's Day.

We got lucky and were able to spend an hour with the lawyer, Mr. Rodriguez. When we came out, we felt armed with what we need to proceed.

But first it was time for Michael's and my Valentine's Day ritual. We shop at Whole Foods for cheese, bread, hummus, fruit, dessert, and flowers. Then we have a picnic, sometimes at a park; this year we chose to have a living room floor picnic. It is one of my favorite things that we do, and it felt nice to have a suspended moment of something nice in the middle of the recent craziness.

Then, back to Ireene. The first step was to get a pre-evaluation of Ireene. An elder care agency interviewed her and gave us a report on Ireene's mental state and well-being. This report tells us whether the evidence supports filing with the court to have a professional guardian appointed for Ireene. The evidence supports it.

When the agency gave me the verbal report, here is what it boiled down to: Ireene still has some energy for a woman who turns 97 in a few months, but she shows signs of extreme paranoia and lack of understanding of health and financial matters. Ireene was welcoming and invited the interviewer in and talked for 30 minutes. The area of concern with that was that she didn't know who the interviewer was and the interviewer did not state a reason for being there. Regardless of that, Ireene was still open to answering questions about money, family, and politics. One of the things the interviewer noted was that Ireene seems to have an exaggerated fixation on shredding. I couldn't help laughing when she told me that. She also had a great deal of anger about "other people" getting a selling appraisal on her house.

She said the appraiser didn't understand that it was a different house from the one that was there before the tornado and should be valued more.

When asked if she'd showered this week, Ireene said no, because it gets water on the floor so she isn't showering. When asked why she doesn't ask the staff to clean up the water, she states that she doesn't like the staff and doesn't want them doing anything for her.

When the interviewer asked Ireene about who is taking care of her bills and her house, Ireene said that her granddaughter is, and then proceeded to say that the granddaughter was also the reason she was there against her will. She also "does not like the granddaughter's personality" but laments that she has no other option but the granddaughter. Ireene wishes that she could have her daughter-in-law, Sarah, take care of things for her, but Sarah is already taking care of Ireene's son, Billy, and Ireene doesn't feel the added burden would be fair to Sarah.

In order to have a professional guardian appointed for Ireene, she would need to be found incompetent to take care of her own affairs. The interviewer believes there is sufficient evidence for this and agrees that filing the Guardianship paperwork is warranted.

Step two, tell Grandma and Uncle Billy.

Forty-Four

Lorna

The day after the paperwork was filed with the court, I talked to Sarah and let her know what was going on. She sounded wary and tired. I told her I'd written a letter to Billy and Ireene so that Sarah did not feel like she had to tell them herself.

Then I dropped this letter in the mailbox, one to Gram and a copy to Uncle Billy.

Dear Gram,

I know we haven't been very successful at having calm conversations lately, and I have some information to share with you, so I thought sending you this might be better. And I want you to have this written down so it will be easier to remember later on.

It has been a hard few months for both of us. I know that you are unhappy with me as your power of attorney/medical representative, but you feel trapped because you have no other option. I have been unhappy because I have tried so hard to follow your doctors' orders, keep your household running, and to arrange your finances so you can live at Sea Breeze, yet you and Uncle Billy have made your displeasure with my actions very clear.

I believe that I should no longer act in a decision-making capacity for you. Everything from medical care to finances to your house has been a battle. It just isn't healthy for either of us to continue in this way. We all know we need to sell your house, but every step in the process seems to raise more anger in you. I don't want to be responsible for such a big decision when all the parts to the decision upset you so.

I love you and have always only wanted to help you, but it is clear to me that the situation we are in isn't working for either of us. As it is right now, it is tearing our family apart. I miss seeing you, but haven't wanted to visit since our last conversation, because we just seem to keep arguing around the same subjects but not getting to any resolutions.

I asked advice of your lawyer, and he referred me to another lawyer who deals with these family situations. There are professional agencies that can take over and be responsible for your finances and major medical decisions. This is the suggested way to go, because they are professionals and have no stake in family matters. Everything they do is run by a judge and monitored by the courts, so there is no worry that they won't act in your best interest. The nurse that came and talked to you from Elder Solutions in February agreed that this is the best way to go.

A panel of interviewers will come over and talk to you soon. Their input will determine whether the outside professional can be appointed to work with you on your behalf. I do not have a date for that yet, but they will call you to set it up.

Hopefully this change will allow you and I to go back to just being granddaughter and grandmother again, and to not have all these other things souring our relationship. As for Uncle Billy's issues, I cannot say whether this process will make him feel better or not. I am solely concerned with making sure you have everything you need and that I stay sane in the process!

Now that the process has begun, my power of attorney is suspended and I will not be able to do anything on your behalf. It will stay that way until a representative is appointed and takes over. I have been keeping up to date with all your bills and they will be fine during the transition.

Hopefully this works well and when we are no longer in the position of me having any say in your living arrangements, maybe we can have a happier relationship again. I think it

will be very nice to have our old
relationship back.

Love,
Lorna

Forty-Five

Lorna

It took almost three weeks to get all three members of the panel to interview Ireene, because apparently they do it one at a time, not in an actual panel. I just got back the evaluations from all three. They believe that Ireene lacks the ability to make informed decisions regarding her rights/ability to: marry, vote, hold a driver's license, travel, seek employment, enter a contract, manage her own property, assist in lawsuits, determine suitable living arrangements, consent to medical treatment, make contracts, deal with payments or debts, and this list went on and on. One even added a footnote that Ireene lacks the rationality to consider her own physical and mental infirmities and determine appropriate living situations.

Reading that report made me feel a thousand times better. With Gram, Uncle Billy, and all of Gram's neighbors so adamant that I was wrong, it felt so good to know that medical professionals saw the same things in Ireene that I see. I knew that copies of the reports were given to Ireene and Uncle Billy, and I wondered if it would have any effect on them. Certainly Michael, Betty, Mom, Aunt Jay, and Uncle John knew that the reports showed an accurate reflection of the situation.

The lawyer, Mr. Rodriguez, got copies of the reports at the same time I did, and his office is drawing up the motion to bring to the court. Once he has filed that motion, he told me, a second lawyer will be appointed to Gram just to go through the process with her and make sure that her best interests are being met. Who gets appointed is purely a matter of who is up next on the court's list of available attorneys.

He said that in situations like this, where the panel was unanimous in saying Ireene would benefit from a professional guardian, the process usually takes just a few weeks. A guardian is identified through the legal system, a court date is set, then the hearing is held to get the judge's ruling.

I feel like I can breathe for the first time in months. Finally we are getting close to a resolution that will keep Gram safe and financially sound, and it will get me out of the firing line with Gram, Billy, and Gram's neighbors. If I hear one more time that the neighbors think Ireene should be allowed to do what she wants, I'm pretty sure I might explode.

Forty-Six

Lorna

For so many years, everywhere I go, I have kept an eye out for things that Gram would like. She loves little gadgets that do interesting things or make things easier for her to do, she loves frogs and little figurines, and she loves anything to do with gardening. So Michael and I usually get things for her, a bag to grow tomatoes upside down in her carport, a salt cellar in the shape of a bird's nest, a device that lets you reseal bags that are usually not re-sealable. She always gets such delight out of them. It's funny, I find that even though things have been so bad lately, I cannot stop myself from wanting to get her nifty gadgets when I see them. And I hope that soon, maybe, things will be calmer so that I can start bringing her things again.

Our court date is scheduled and I've already made plans to be out of work for the day to attend. I've heard that Gram's neighbors are rallying the neighborhood to go to court on her behalf and tell the judge that she is just fine to live on her own (I'd love to know what they are basing that opinion on). I'm hoping that the judge puts more stock in the reports of a doctor, a nurse, and a social worker than in the opinions of some nosy neighbors. But I am not looking forward to having me and Mr. Rodriguez on one side of the room and Ireene's entire neighborhood on the other. Well, really it would be me, Michael, Mr. Rodriguez, and Jay and John, but the scenario I'm picturing in my head is not pretty. I have no idea what the courtroom will look like, but I picture everything in muted tones and beiges with mahogany wood everywhere.

Though the thought of the court date makes me a little ill, in general, I haven't felt this calm in months. I haven't painted in a long time, and I'm starting to think about what my next piece might be. I had time to pay my own bills and go through old stacks of mail. My eyelid actually stopped twitching for an hour or so yesterday, which makes me feel much less crazy.

After dinner, Michael and I take our dog for a walk. Walks with her are never very far anymore, because her little old legs hurt. She still has enough energy to think she can chase squirrels though. The squirrels must be able to sense she is really no threat, because they don't even bother to run. Afterward, I settle on the couch with the dog next to me and check my email. I wish I could stop checking email so often, and think there are only a few more weeks until I should stop getting distressing emails all the time. I see one in my Inbox from Mr. Rodriguez.

Hoping he is giving me directions for the hearing, I click open the email. My hopes fall when I read that the lawyer that was appointed to Gram is challenging the findings of the panel and wants Ireene evaluated by his own doctor. Since he cannot possibly make that happen in time for the hearing, the hearing must be postponed. I quickly fire back an email asking if they can force the lawyer to schedule the appointment before the hearing so everything can stay on schedule. I know the answer will be no, but I have to try.

I want to scream. Are you kidding me? Three (really four if you count the pre-evaluation) health care professionals agreed that Ireene needs a guardian, but he is still going to question that!? So much for the end being in sight. Michael and I are planning a trip up north soon and now that I'm worried the postponed court date will conflict with that. Why can't anything be simple?

Forty-Seven

Lorna

After several weeks of "scheduling conflicts", Gram's lawyer's doctor evaluated Gram. I received a letter that said they would be holding the findings confidential. They may as well just say, "Our doctor agreed with your panel!" There would be no other reason for them the hide the findings. I try not to feel smug about it, but the petty side of me wants to say a big "I told you so". Since that would probably not help my situation, I figure I'll keep mum on that one. The next step is to reschedule the court date.

Smartly, I think, I didn't let it get my hopes up now that their evaluation is finished. Or I thought I didn't. But when Sarah called, I realized that I had been harboring some hope that this would soon come to an end. That is why when she said, "I've talked to Ireene and she agreed to let me be her guardian," I almost let loose a string of expletives that would have made any truck driver proud.

"Are you serious, Sarah? Why would you do this now when we were so close to bringing this whole debacle to an end?" I asked her. I can feel the tears starting to burn in the back of my eyes.

"Ireene just seems so sad. I think she is depressed and all of this is making her worse. I thought this way you could be done with it, but she would be happy," Sarah replied.

I say, "I'm guessing you mean she would be happy because as her guardian, you would just let her move home to her house where everyone agrees she isn't safe."

"Well. Yeah. That is what she wants. She is so unhappy!"

"And when she cuts her leg on something and bleeds to death?" I ask heartlessly.

"Well...She seems so depressed that I thought it would

be better for her to be home and happy for a little while than in Sea Breeze and safe but unhappy," Sarah answers.

"I'm sorry, what? You'd rather her be happy than safe?"

"Yes," Sarah responds. I think about that for a minute and realize that probably a lot of people would agree with that. Let her die happy. The only problem with that is that I didn't sign a legal document that said I'd help her be happy. I signed one that said I'd help her be safe and keep her finances secure. I tell that to Sarah.

Then I say, "Of course she agreed to let you be her guardian, because you just caved and said you'd give her whatever she wants! Is that reasonable to you to give a person who has just been identified as incompetent by a panel of health professionals whatever they want?"

"I know," Sarah says. "I just can't stand for everyone to be like this and I thought if I offered, that it would help."

"Sarah, you're killin' me. Why couldn't you just have let it finish and let the professional guardian be appointed? That is the whole point of a professional guardian...they can't be swayed or manipulated by either the incompetent nonagenarians, a husband with a screw loose, or anyone else in the family.

"Alright, I need to think about this. I'll give you a call tomorrow okay?" I ask.

"Yes," Sarah replies.

I hang up and cry in earnest. I can't take any more of this. I hate all of it so much that I wish I could just give it all up and let them all do whatever the heck they want. I call Betty and fill her in. For as overwhelmed as I am, Betty is as mad. She says that the part of the family that turned on me these last few months is now trying to take control and let her grandmother die. I'm too tired to think about it now and I tell her I need to go to bed. That has been my coping mechanism since I was a child - too stressed out? Go to sleep. Betty knows that about me and lets me off the phone. I tell Michael I'm going to bed early and I go curl up in our room in the dark.

I wake up in the morning to a text from sometime the night before from Betty that says, "I chewed Uncle Billy out. Didn't mean to but it just happened."

Forty-Eight

Lorna

After Betty's "conversation" with Uncle Billy, Sarah let me know that she decided not to try to become Ireene's guardian. She said that she'd offered as a way to try to help, but since everyone seemed opposed, she now thinks it is a bad idea. Billy, who was on a madding rant before is now completely unhinged and wants Betty and I, and Jay for that matter, to stay away from his mother. I guess it would be moot to point out that I've been *trying* to "stay away" from his mother, but the lawyer's postponement is making that impossible.

I learned from Sarah that Ireene had a friend take her to a department store where she tried to use her credit card and it was declined. As I'd told her in my letter, the bills were paid up so that they would not become overdue in the two to three weeks the original court date was supposed to take. Since her attorney postponed, and I no longer have power of attorney to sign checks, her bills are going unpaid while he is messing around with extra expert opinions.

I'm starting to get the same dread of opening emails now that I'm dealing with lawyer stuff that I did with my phone when Gram and Billy were calling me with their daily craziness. As I open this one, all I can do is sigh. Mr. Rodriguez reports that Gram's lawyer is alleging financial misconduct on my part and would like copies of everything I've done since October.

I lean back in my chair and let out a frustrated breath. Then meanly, I start to smile. He asked for it! I am now so glad that I kept a copy of every letter, bill, check, and receipt for everything Ireene-related. And it is not a small amount. I am one of those people who pays *everything* online. Before this, I don't think I'd written a check other than for rent in years. But Ireene pays everything with a check- six credit cards, gas bill, water bill, car insurance, medical bills, home owners' insurance, pool (and we know how that turned out!), lawn, and about a zillion other things. So if her lawyer would like copies, I am so happy to give him copies of everything.

Forty-Nine

Lorna

Now that I am learning how this goes, I don't drop off the copies at Gram's lawyer's office. I drop them off at Mr. Rodriguez's office, so his secretary can inventory everything before they courier it over. She laughs as I drop two full file boxes of copies on the floor, "*How* many months has it been?" she asked.

"Well, I figured he'd want me to be thorough. I even copied my entries in her check register for him."

"That is probably good," she replied, "because he has also contacted the financial advisor you have your grandmother's stocks with to request a detailed account of all activities." Of course he did.

"You know what? That is fine. He is going to find the same level of detail there that he is getting here. So let him have at it."

Fifty

Lorna

I have to admit, I thought I was starting to get numb to Gram's lawyer's foolishness. I haven't heard anything about the finances in several days, so I guess he just dropped that idea when he realized there wasn't anything there to find fault with.

But my phone rang at work just now and when I answered, I heard the manager from Sea Breeze and she was totally hysterical.

"I just opened a letter from a lawyer that says Sea Breeze is holding Ireene against her will because she doesn't have the code to the security gate. None of the patients have the code to the security gate!" she says.

"Ok," I say. "What is he getting at? What does he want now?"

"He says we are to give her the code to the security gate by 5 pm today or he will file charges of unlawful imprisonment against the administration of Sea Breeze." Her voice is getting shrill now.

She continues, "We can't have this! I just had to fax this to my Risk Management office and I think they might make me discharge Ireene."

"Alright. This isn't the first thing this lawyer has tried. Let me give you the fax number of my lawyer. Fax him over the letter and I'll call him. One of us will call you back and tell you what to do."

I give her the fax number and we hang up. I don't doubt that they'll consider asking Ireene to leave. She has caused them so many problems in such a short amount of time. If I had to bet, I would say she acts outrageously on purpose so they will kick her out, because she thinks that will make it so she can go home. I get back on the phone with Mr.

Rodriguez's office, talk to his secretary. He is out of the office, but she'll find him and they will follow up. She assures me that since it is mentioned in the intake paperwork for all residents that there is a coded gate for the security of residents who have diminished mental capacity, that there is probably not grounds for what Ireene's lawyer is trying.

It is getting close to the end of my work day and I wonder if I will ever have a normal day again.

In the morning, I check in with Mr. Rodriguez and he says he talked to Sea Breeze and to Ireene's lawyer and not to worry about any of this, that it will likely just go away. That is what he thought.

I'm still worried about the possibility of them booting Ireene out. If they say they are going to, maybe I can convince them to let her stay just until the new guardian is appointed, so that person can be responsible for determining where Ireene goes from here.

Fifty-One

Lorna

I would laugh at the absurdity of this if it wasn't upping my chances of needing a padded room. Gram's lawyer wants to know why I haven't been paying her bills? The day before my power of attorney was revoked in February, I had Ireene's mail forwarded, with agreement from Mr. Rodriguez, to her at her Assisted Living Facility. I was no longer to be responsible for her bills and legal affairs, so there was no longer a reason for her mail to come to my house.

Ireene had not, however, begun paying them when they started arriving at her apartment. So from the time that I originally filed the guardianship papers, through her lawyer's gyrations with expert evaluations, alleged financial misconduct, and screwing with Sea Breeze over the locked gate, she had not kept up with her bills. Now her credit card being declined makes even more sense. I take this as just one more representation of the fact that she should not be handling her own affairs, but what do I know? Besides that, Mr. Rodriguez informed her lawyer at the time that her mail was being forwarded to her, so shouldn't he have wondered about this sometime earlier?

The fact that he now wants to know why I haven't been paying her bills is laughable. When I relay the reasons, the response he comes back with is to say that he will have Ireene reinstate my Power of Attorney so that I can resume paying her bills.

"Soooooo… a few days ago you were alleging financial misconduct against me and trying to prove that I'd mishandled and misused Ireene's money. And now you suddenly trust me again and want me to pay her bills? Pay her bills, mind you, while you go through this list of things that continues to postpone our court date. I think I'll have to decline your request."

Fifty-Two

Lorna

Michael and I just left Jay and John's house. They had us over for dinner to talk about things, and now we're heading home. Since we've been in this thing together, I wanted to talk to them about my plans.

And my plans are this: tomorrow I will go see Mr. Rodriguez, bring him a box of any remaining miscellaneous items I have of Ireene's, and tell him that I would like to drop the attempt to have a professional guardian appointed for Ireene. I will tell him that I do not want my Power of Attorney reinstated, and ask him to please deliver the box and relay this information to Ireene's lawyer.

Day before yesterday I finally hit my limit. I think Michael had hit his long ago, but was riding it out with me. But he is more than happy for me to end this now.

My grandmother is trying to have me charged with unlawful imprisonment.

I keep saying it over in my head, like somehow I can make it not be true, "My grandmother is trying to charge me with unlawful imprisonment."

I know Mr. Rodriguez will say that they have no grounds, that if we just wait a little longer, everything is on our side and we will eventually win and the court will appoint Ireene a professional guardian. And I just don't care. I cannot do this for one more minute.

I guess when their attempt to strong-arm the Assisted Living Facility fizzled out, they decided I might be a better target. Probably her lawyer figures if he throws enough bullshit at me, eventually I'll cave and give up. He was right.

I doubt it could have been my grandmother's idea, but I guess I'll never really know that. But whether or not it was her idea, she still agreed and signed off on having me served with papers that threatened to charge me with a felony.

I know her mental state is altered. I know she was oxygen-deprived for much too long and the woman that came out on the other side of it was not my normal grandmother. I know my true grandmother would not consider such a thing. But this grandmother did. And this grandmother is the one that I must, after almost a year, stop fighting to take care of.

Epilogue

Ireene

I thought I'd be happy to be home, and I guess I am. Looking at the calendar I think I've been home about three months now. I still feel angry all the time. Everyone keeps trying to come in and unpack the boxes that are all over the floor that my granddaughter packed all my belongings in. I don't need their help! I'll get to the boxes when I get to them. Even the Christmas tree is down out of the attic. I think it might take me a few more weeks before my legs are strong enough to climb up and put it back in the attic.

My neighbor, Willa, isn't here; she lives back east most of the year. Her house is dark now. The neighbor on my other side is supposed to be taking me to doctors' appointments and helping me with my bills. He hasn't come around in a few days, I don't think. He's been getting so bossy that I'd rather him not be here much. He is always getting on me about taking my pills. I told him I don't need his help.

Most days I spend sitting at my dining room table. I look at magazines. I shred old papers. I can't really read much anymore, but I can still write cards most days. So I keep up. I keep the lights off because I know I can't afford the light bill. And I keep the curtains closed and the doors locked.

Billy and Sarah bring my dog, Mars, to visit. But Mars doesn't seem interested in me anymore. He used to follow me around wherever I went. Now he just sniffs and goes off to a corner to sleep.

A little while ago Meals on Wheels dropped off some food for my weekend. It is Friday afternoon, so they gave me stuff for the next couple of days. I get up from the dining room table and walk in to the kitchen to get my dinner. I open a cabinet and pull out a plate, then go to the refrigerator to pick something out of what food they've left for me. I turn back around to reach for the plate and hit my head on the open cabinet door. The next thing I know I'm on the floor and I can't tell what hurts the most.

I must have gotten my head but good because I feel blood running down my face. I try to get up so I can get something to stop the bleeding and the pain is unbearable. I think my hip cracked again, but the pain seems even worse than last time, and I didn't think that was possible. I must have hit my elbow on the way down because it not only feels broken, but there is a large patch of skin hanging off from my elbow down the back of my forearm, and it is bleeding profusely.

I think I might have blacked out for a minute, because I look around me now and there is a growing puddle of blood. Between my hip and my elbow, I can't seem to move enough in any direction to get a hold of something to pull myself up. The only thing in my reach is the trash can. I try to reach it with my right arm but can't support myself on my left arm enough to be able to reach in to see if I can grab an old paper towel or napkin to use as a compress.

I think back to my ambulance days and know I have to try to stop the bleeding. I can see the clock over the microwave from here. Four-thirty. What day is it again? Friday, I think. I try to pull part of my shirt around to my elbow to stop the bleeding but I don't really have anything to put on my head. I press my hand on it and try to apply pressure.

I lay back on the tile as that is all I can think of to do. I know I should keep my wounds above my heart, but I don't feel strong enough.

I keep hoping someone will come and help me. It has gotten very dark and the clock shows 9:33 pm. I've been laying here for hours and the pain is making me nauseous. Maybe my neighbors will see that my lights are not on when they usually are at night. All the blinds are pulled tight, so they won't be able to see me through the window. I know someone will come though. I search for my necklace alarm before I remember that it was a long time ago that I had one of those.

Henry is sitting with me now waiting. He is sure someone will come too. He tells me it is almost morning. I've so missed him and want to talk to him but I hurt so much I can't focus on a conversation. I don't think I've been sleeping because I wouldn't be able to sleep through these stabbing sensations, but I seem to have lost some of the night anyway. As it starts to get light, I renew my efforts to try to move. My hands are sticky with blood from my head. The flow is much weaker now than it was last night. My blood thinners never let my blood clot all the way. I try to drag myself across the floor to reach the door, but my bloody hand slips and I go back down on my elbow. Oh do I howl at that.

I feel hungry and remember that I never got to eat dinner last night. It would normally be time to eat breakfast now. I feel so tired and wonder if Sarah was planning to bring Billy by to see me this weekend? Maybe she told me, but I can't remember. I keep squinting at the clock willing someone to come, but it is harder to see now. It must be because I'm tired that my eyes are getting fuzzy. I lay my head back down, close my eyes to take a rest, and listen hoping to hear a car in the driveway.

15954676R00072

Made in the USA
Lexington, KY
28 June 2012